COMICS LAND

by
STONE ARCH
BOOKS

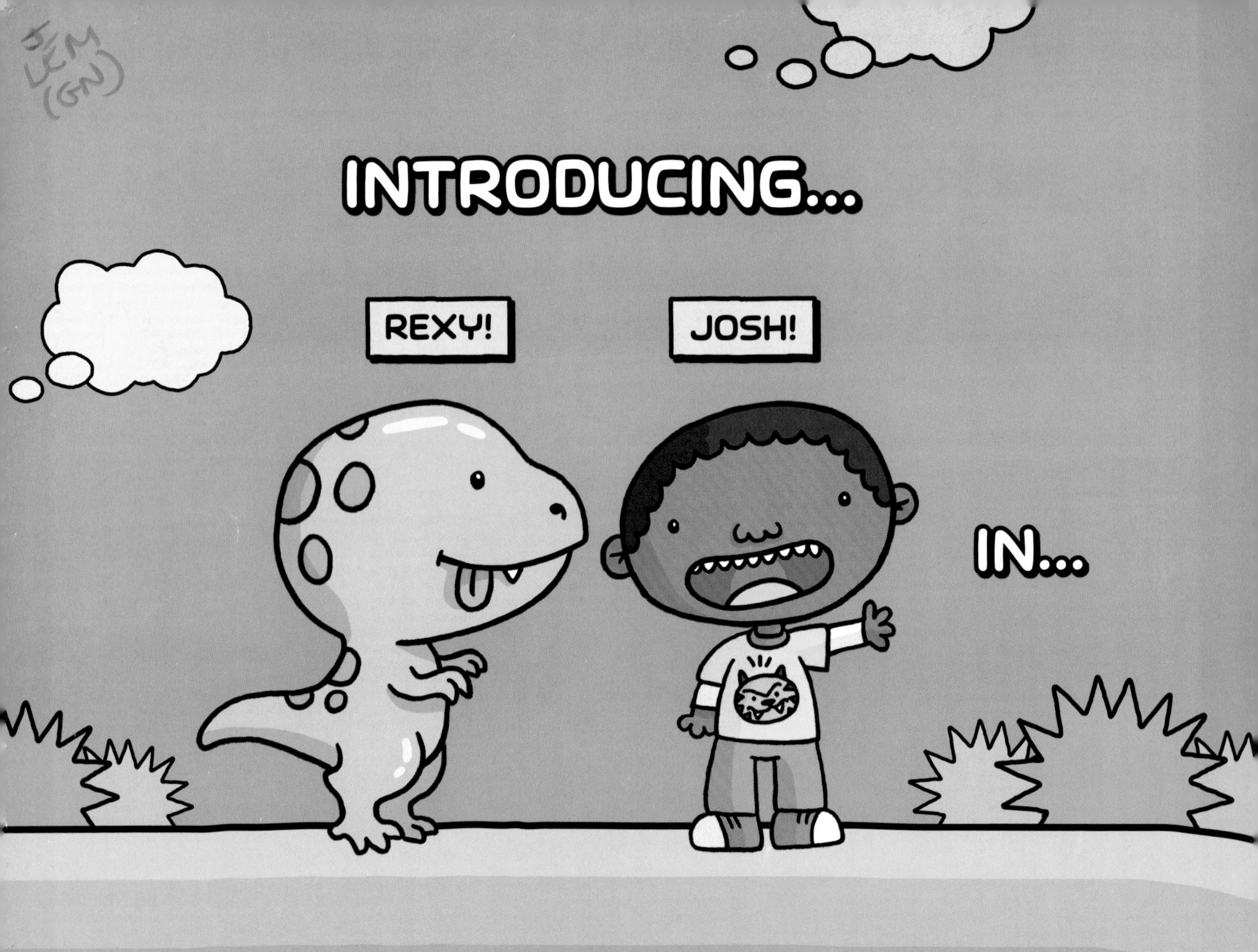
INTRODUCING...
REXY!
JOSH!
IN...

STONE ARCH BOOKS™
www.capstonepub.com

1710 Roe Crest Drive, North Mankato, Minnesota 56003

Cataloging-in-Publication data is available on the Library of Congress website.
ISBN: 978-1-4342-4270-9 (hardcover) • ISBN: 978-1-4342-4029-3 (library binding)

Printed in United States of America in Brainderd, Minnesota. 092012 006938BANGS13

DINOSAURS FOR BREAKFAST

written by
AMY J. LEMKE

illustrated by
JESS BRADLEY

designed by
BOB LENTZ

edited by
JULIE GASSMAN

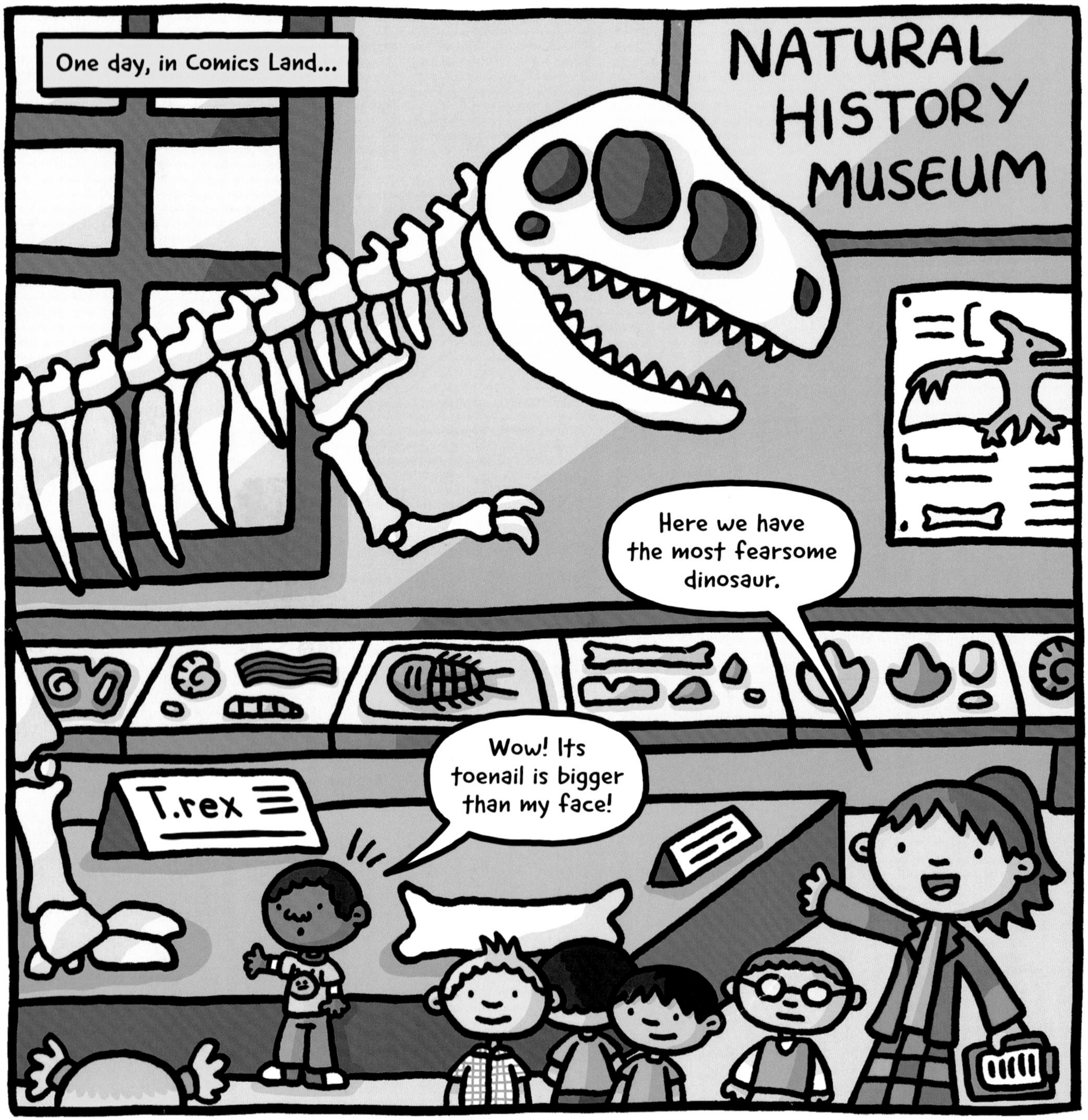
One day, in Comics Land...
NATURAL HISTORY MUSEUM
Here we have the most fearsome dinosaur.
T.rex
Wow! Its toenail is bigger than my face!

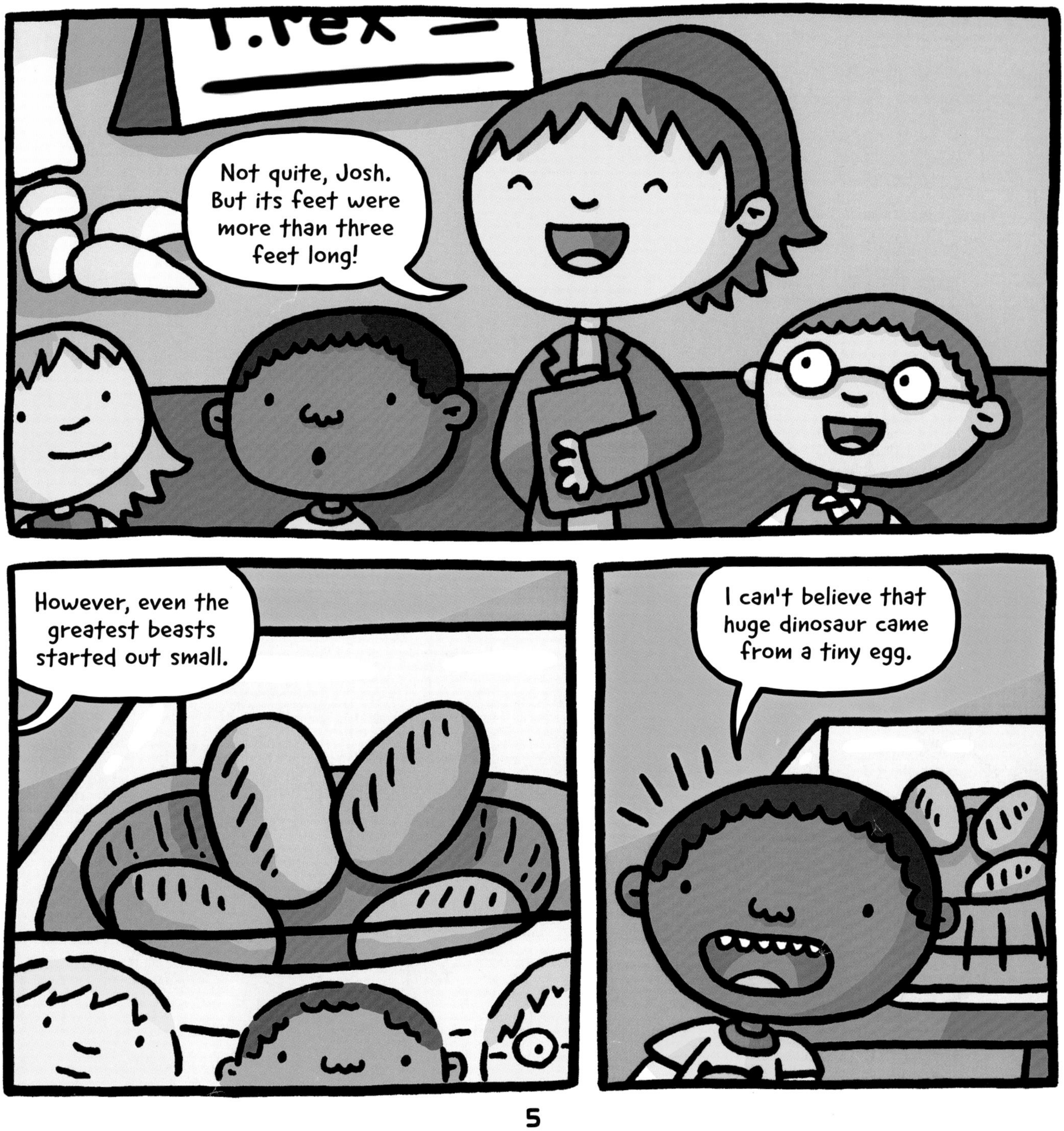
T.rex
Not quite, Josh. But its feet were more than three feet long!
However, even the greatest beasts started out small.
I can't believe that huge dinosaur came from a tiny egg.

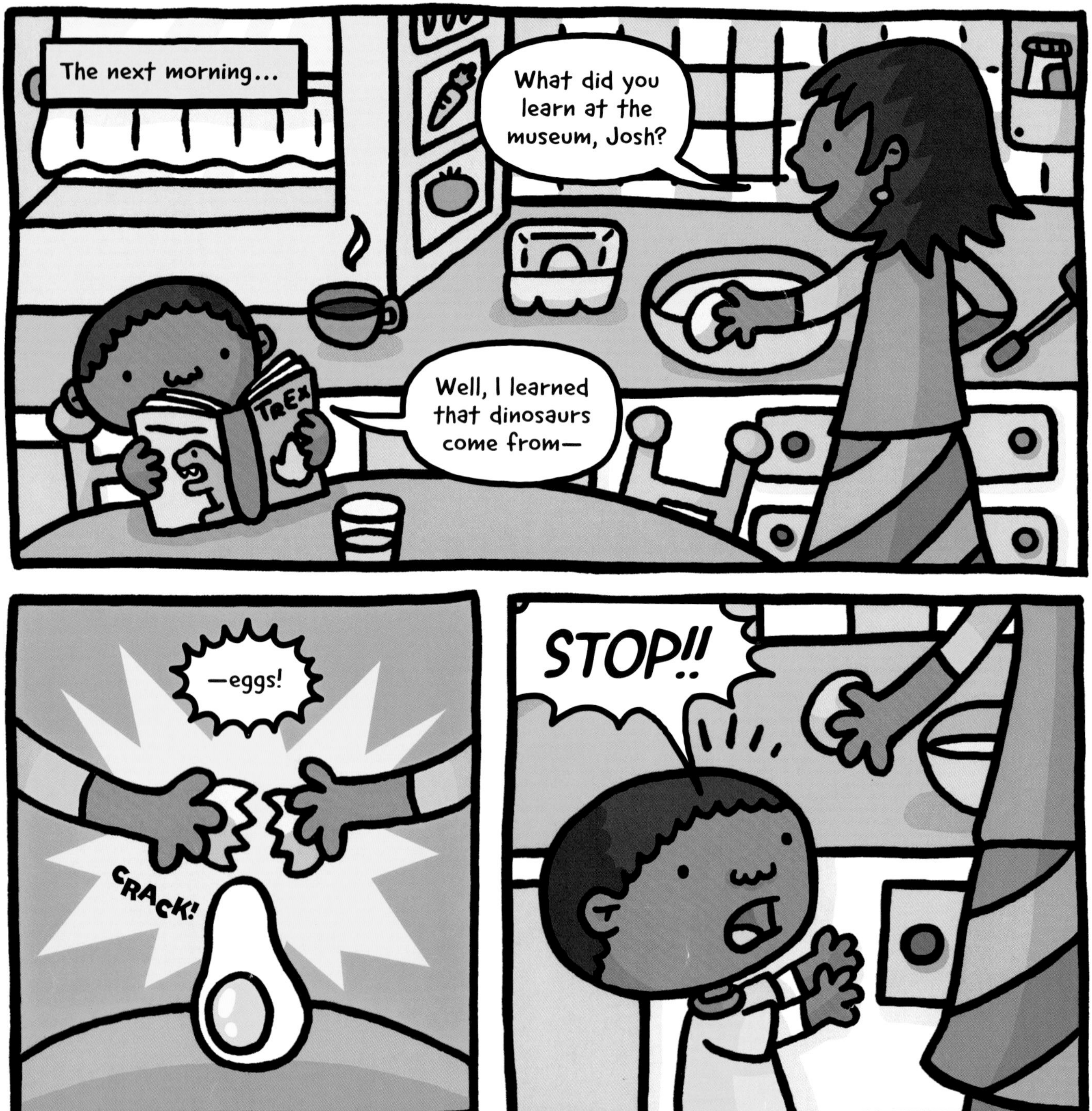
The next morning...
What did you learn at the museum, Josh?
Well, I learned that dinosaurs come from—
TREX
—eggs!
CRACK!
STOP!!

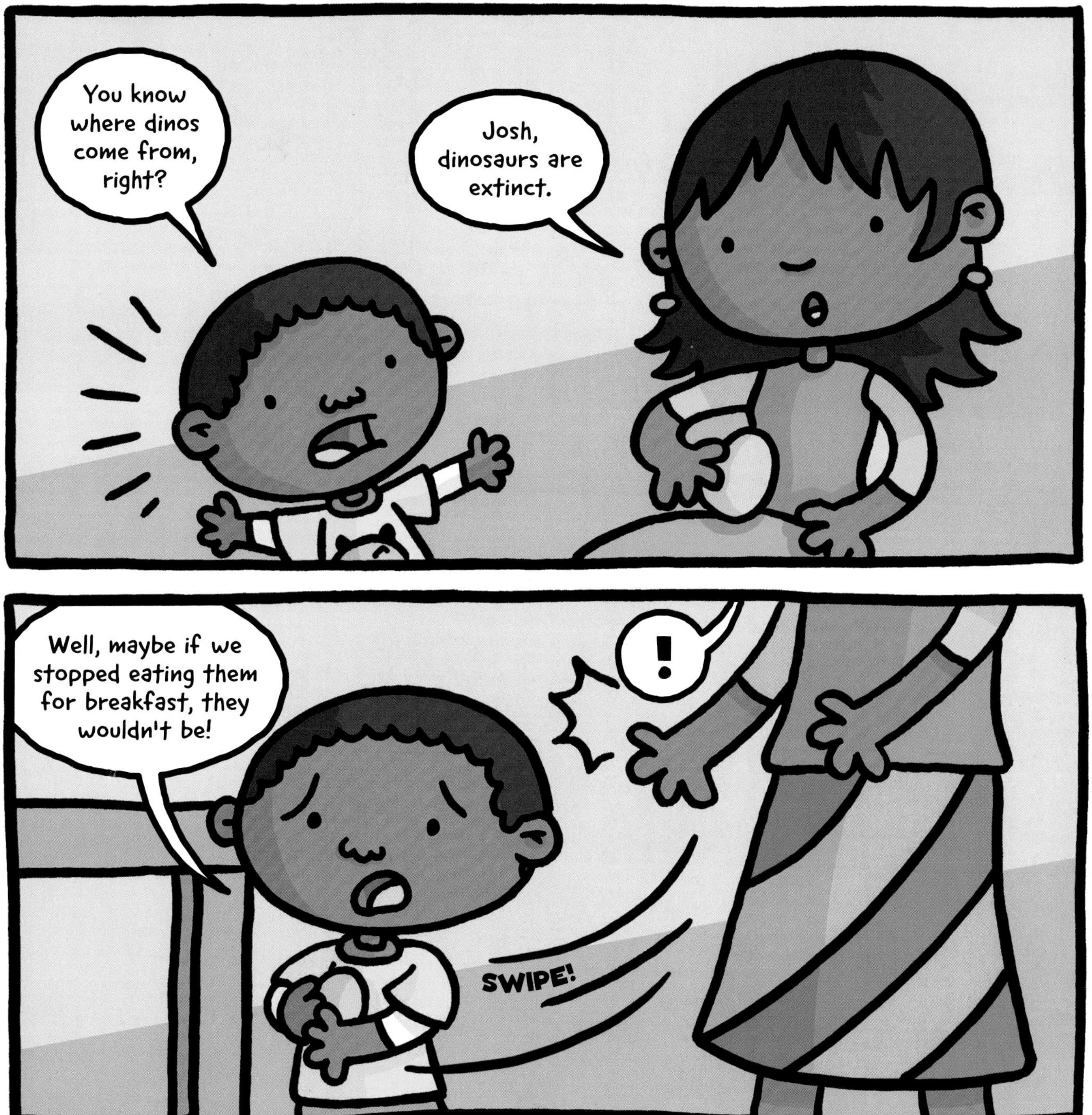
You know where dinos come from, right?
Josh, dinosaurs are extinct.
Well, maybe if we stopped eating them for breakfast, they wouldn't be!
!
SWIPE!

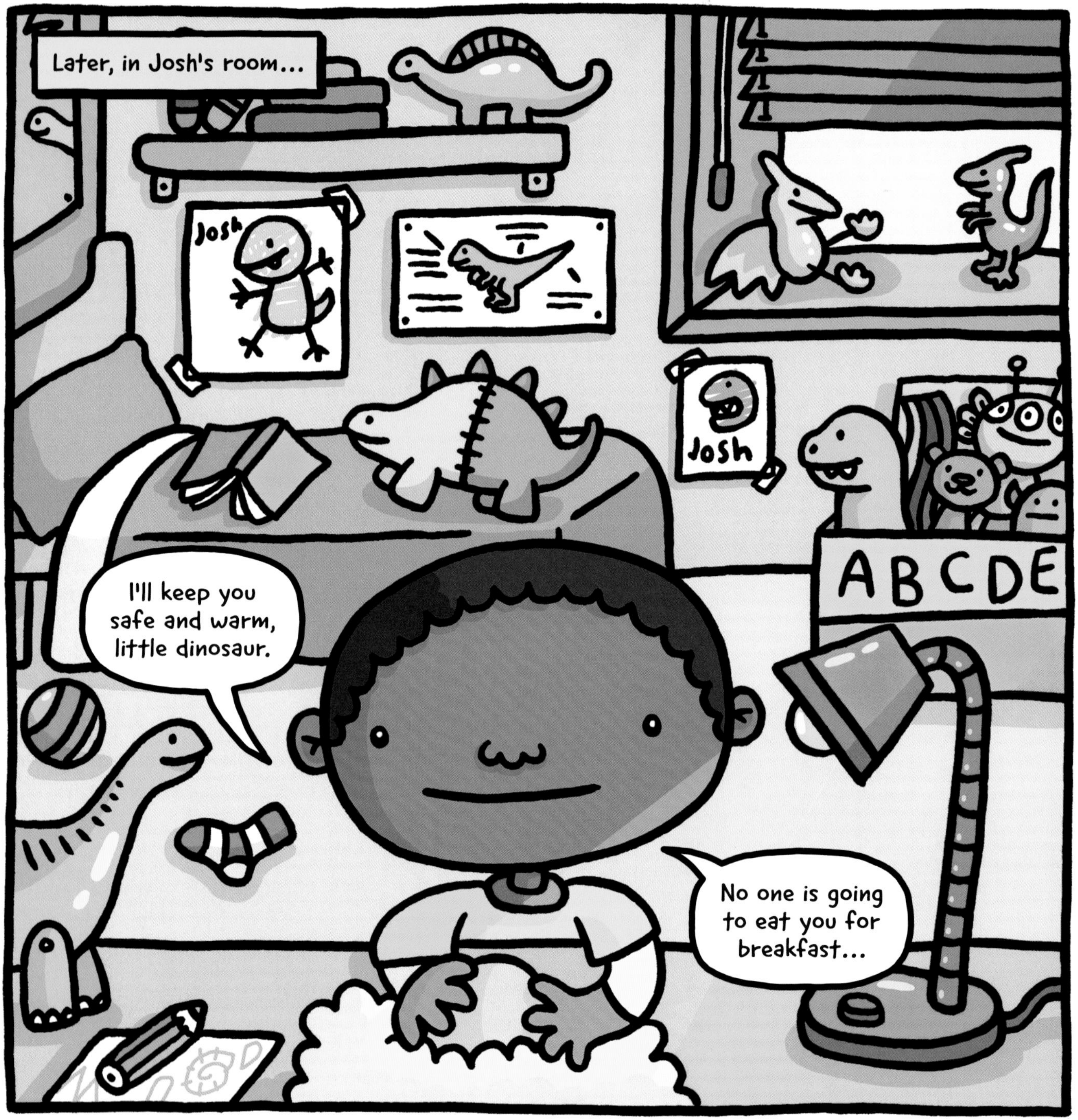
Later, in Josh's room...
Josh
Josh
ABCDE
I'll keep you safe and warm, little dinosaur.
No one is going to eat you for breakfast...

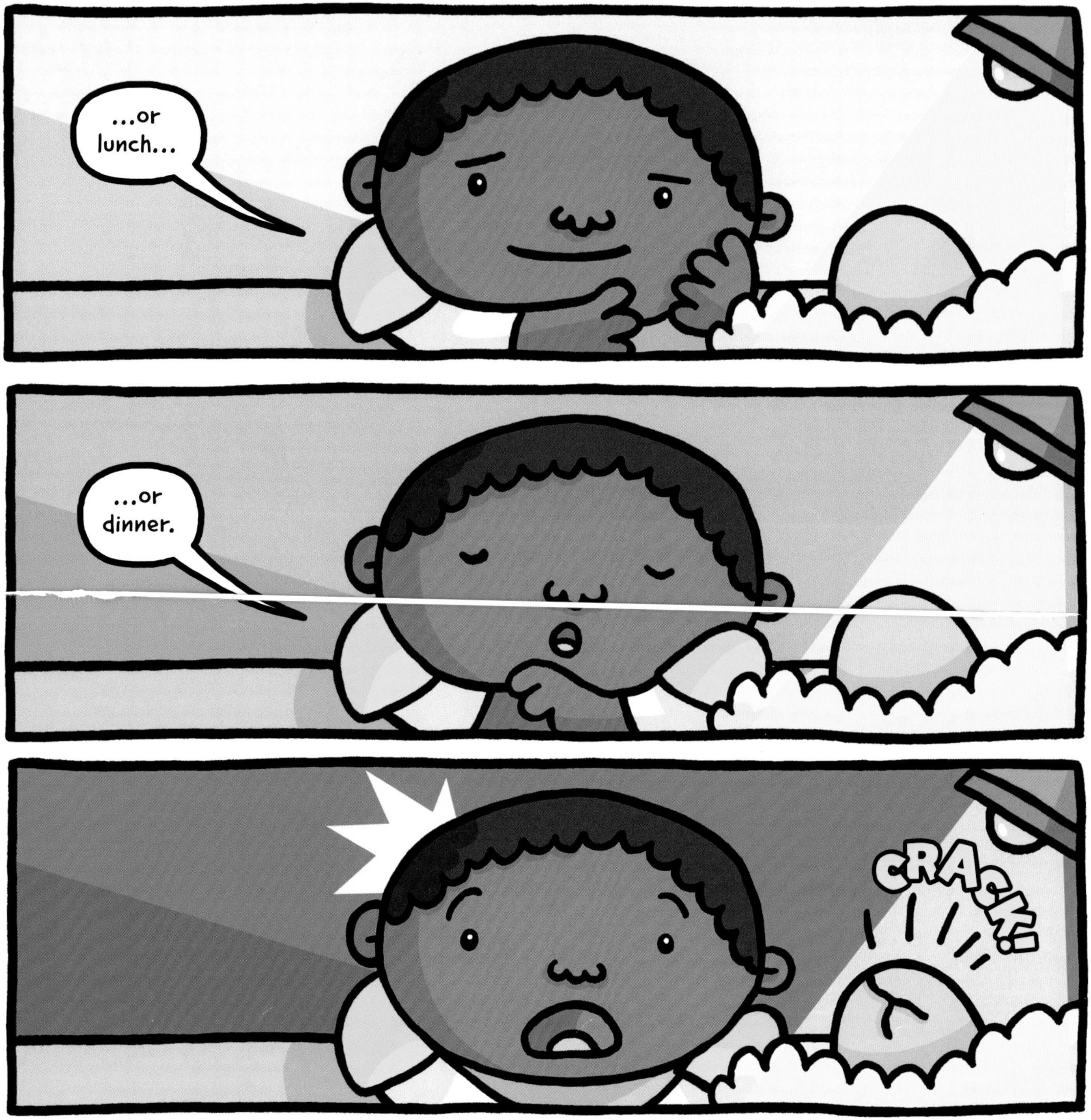
...or lunch...
...or dinner.
CRACK!

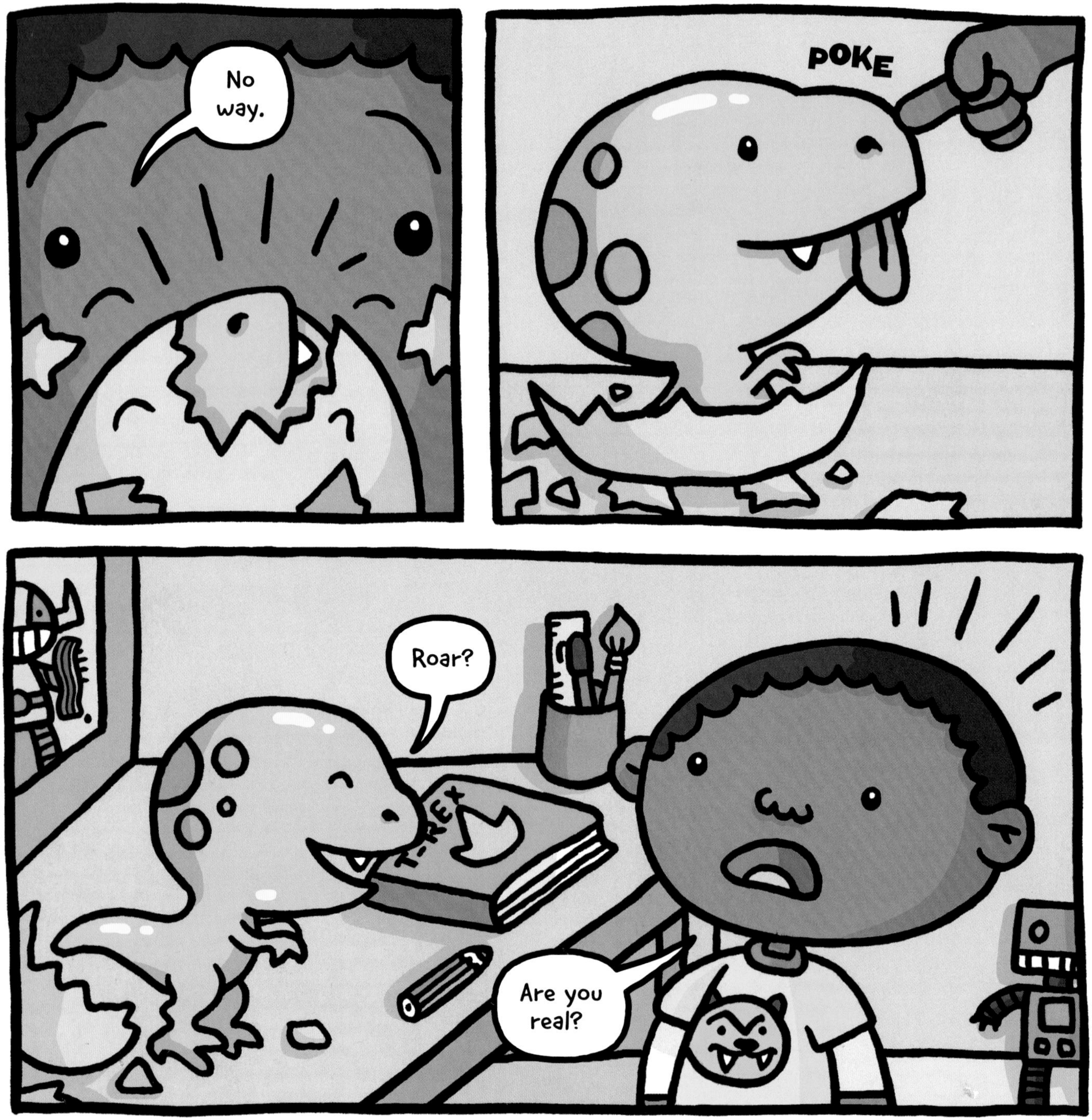
No way.
POKE
Roar?
T-REX
Are you real?

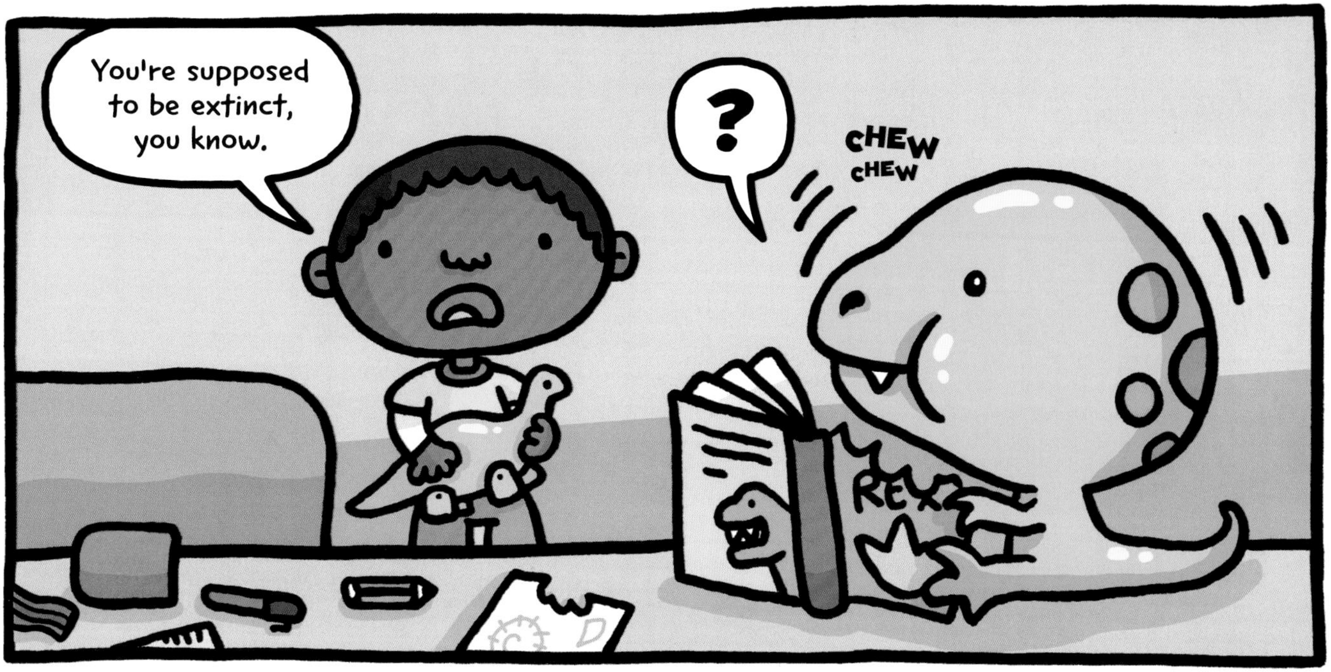
You're supposed to be extinct, you know.
?
CHEW CHEW
REX

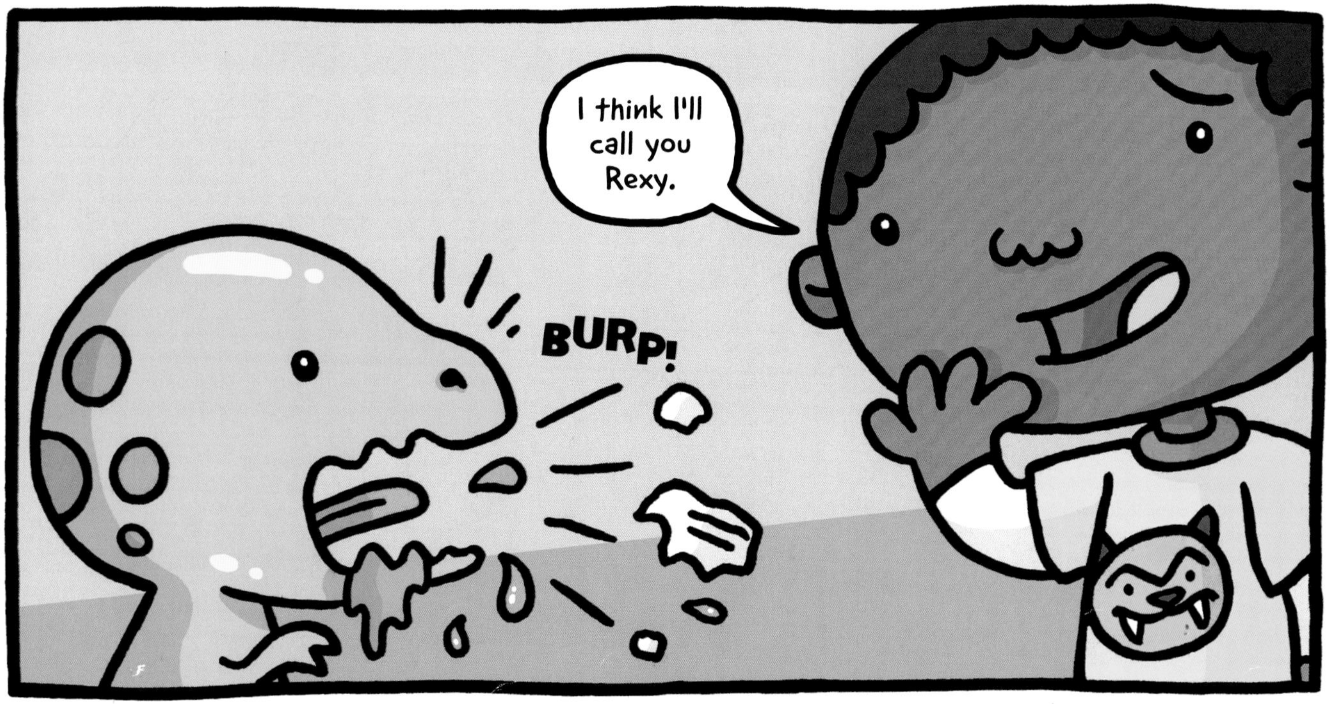
I think I'll call you Rexy.
BURP!

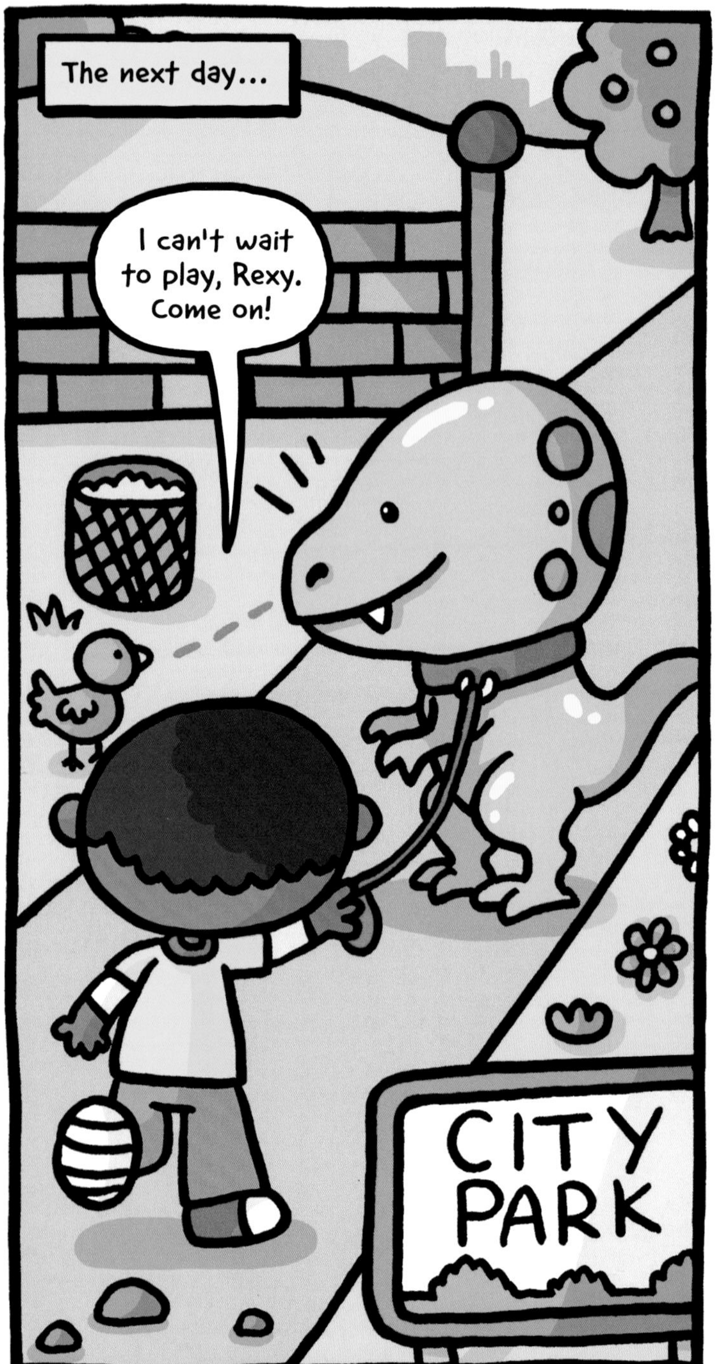
The next day...
I can't wait to play, Rexy. Come on!
CITY PARK

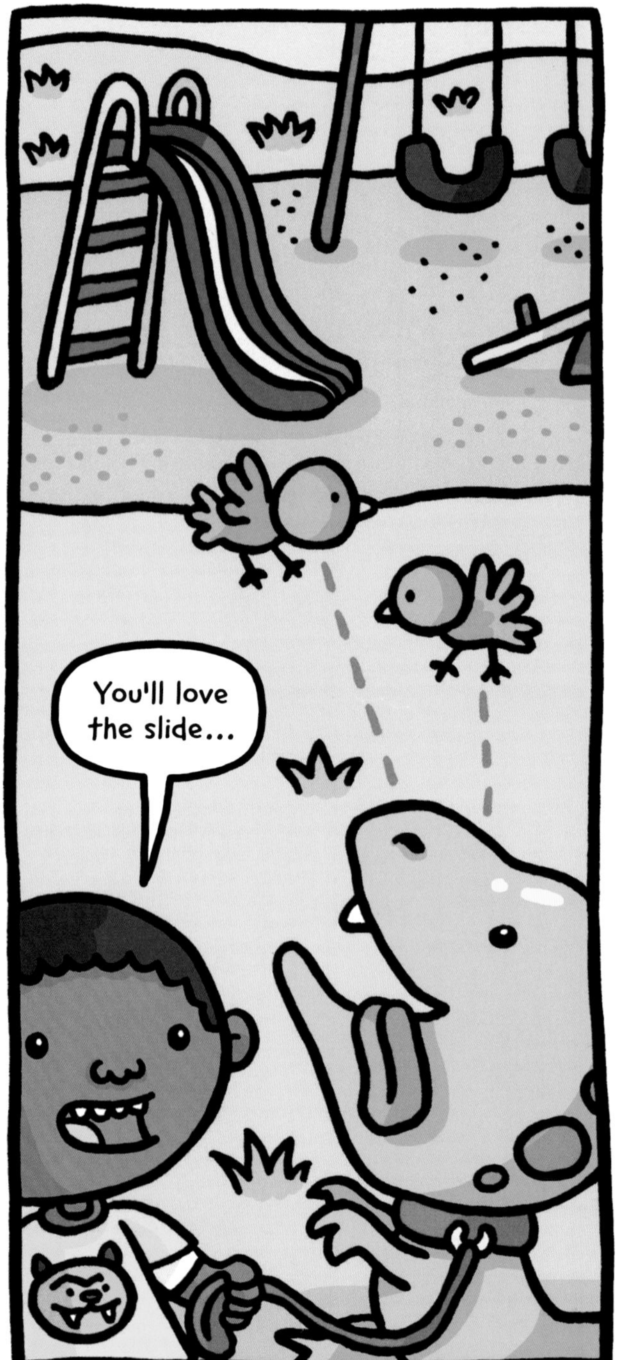
You'll love the slide...

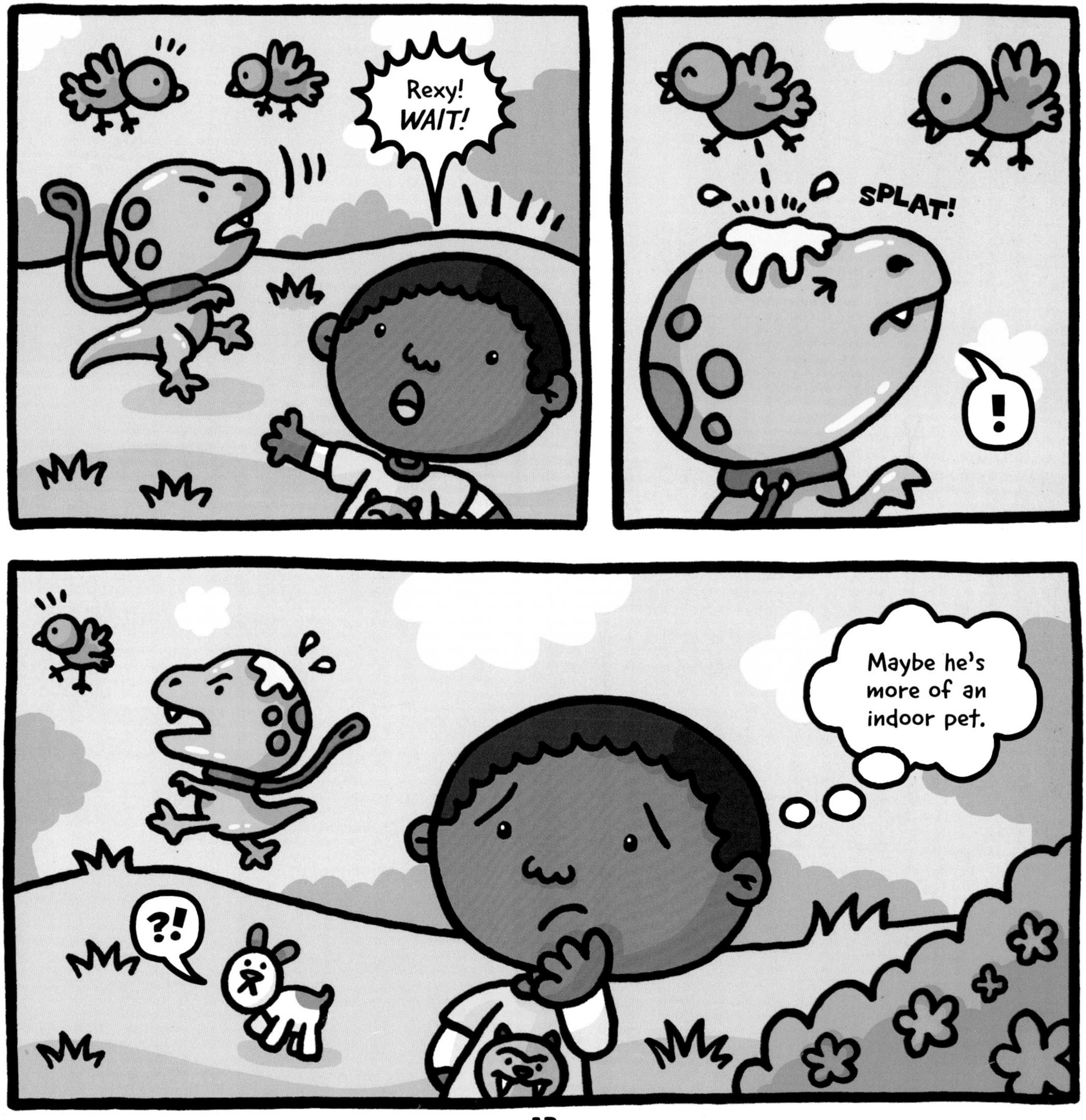
Rexy! WAIT!
SPLAT!
!
Maybe he's more of an indoor pet.
?!

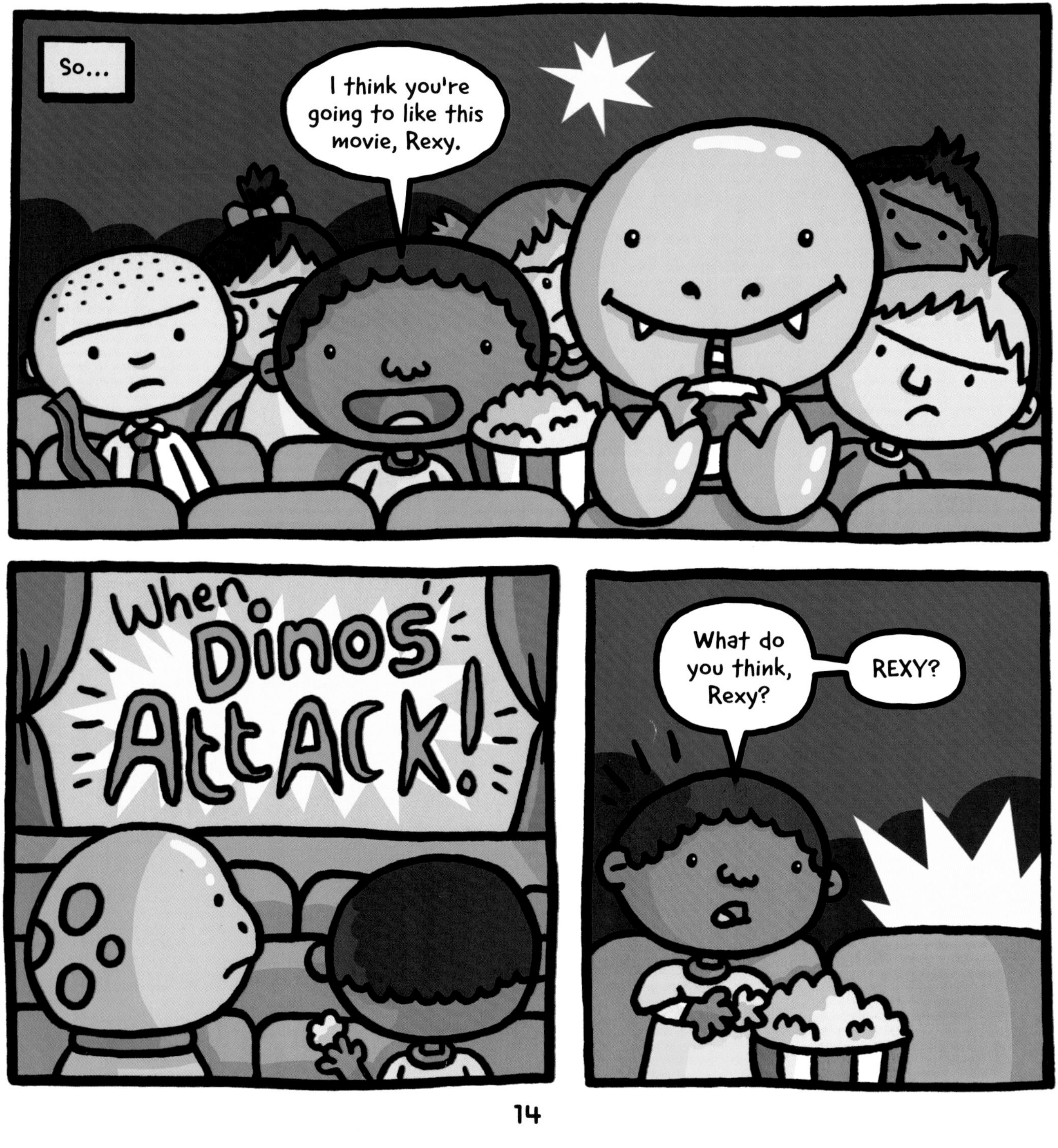
So...
I think you're going to like this movie, Rexy.
When Dinos Attack!
What do you think, Rexy?
REXY?

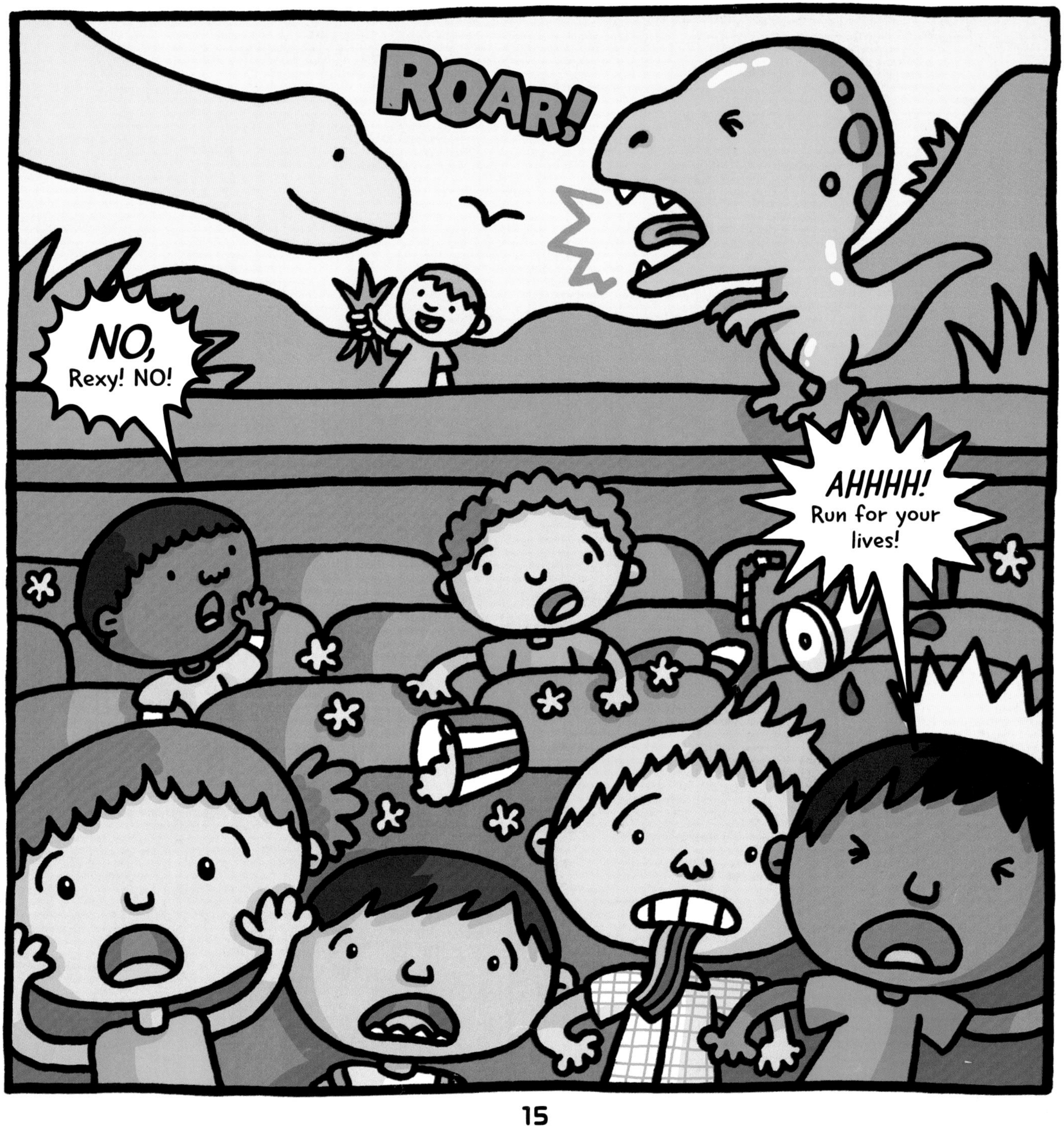
ROAR!
NO, Rexy! NO!
AHHHH! Run for your lives!

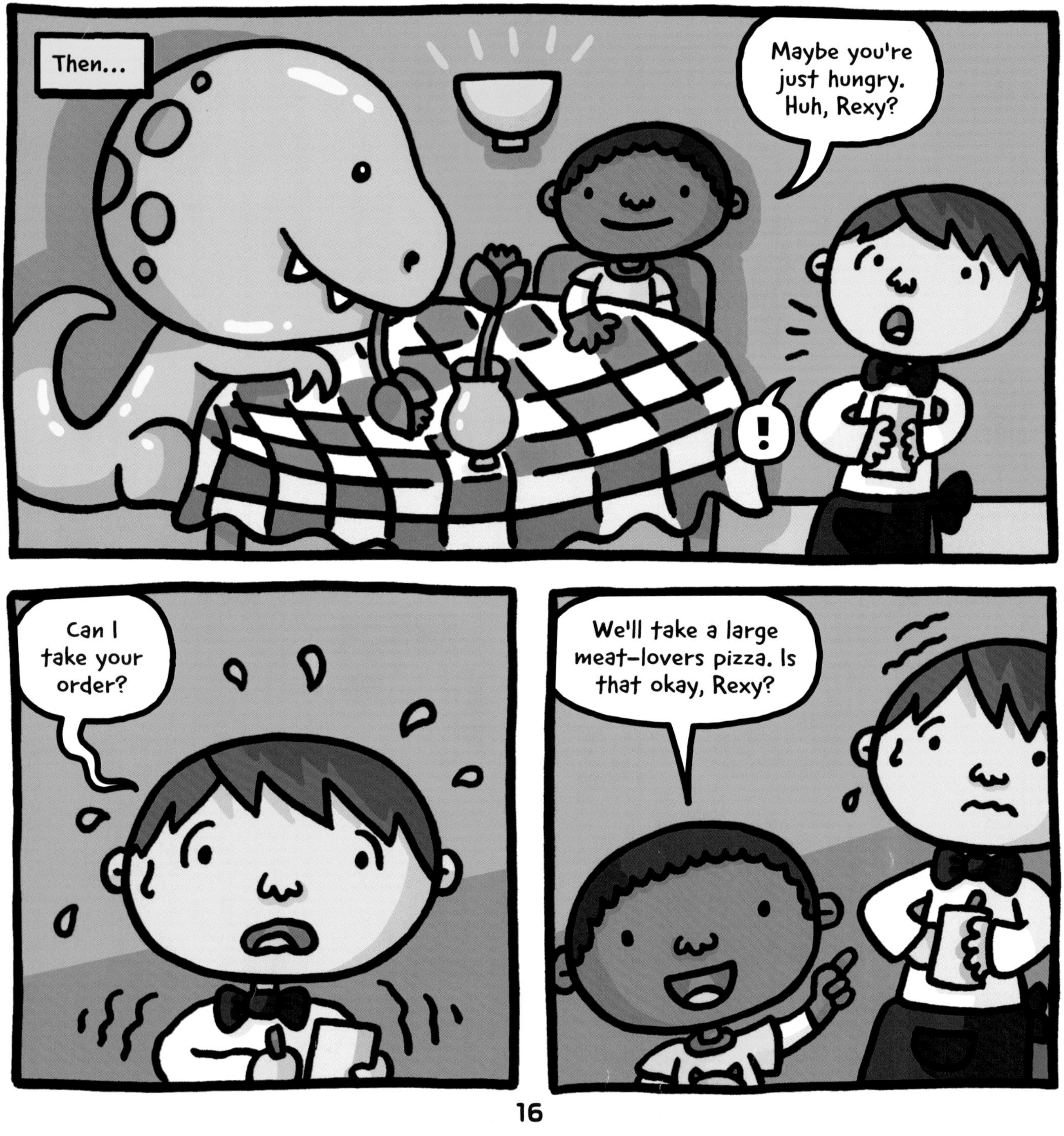
Then...
Maybe you're just hungry. Huh, Rexy?
!
Can I take your order?
We'll take a large meat-lovers pizza. Is that okay, Rexy?

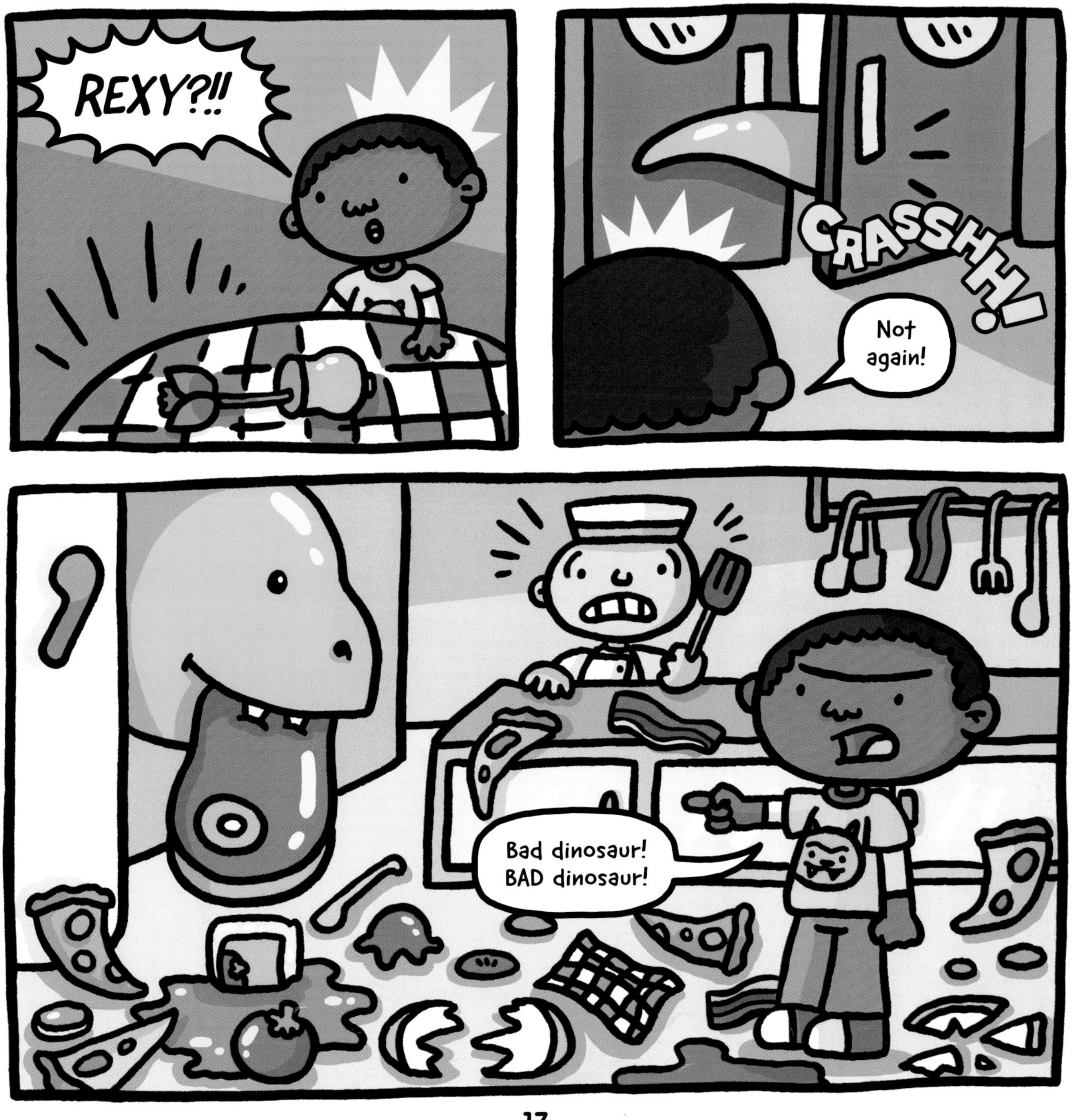
REXY?!!
CRASSHH!
Not again!
Bad dinosaur! BAD dinosaur!

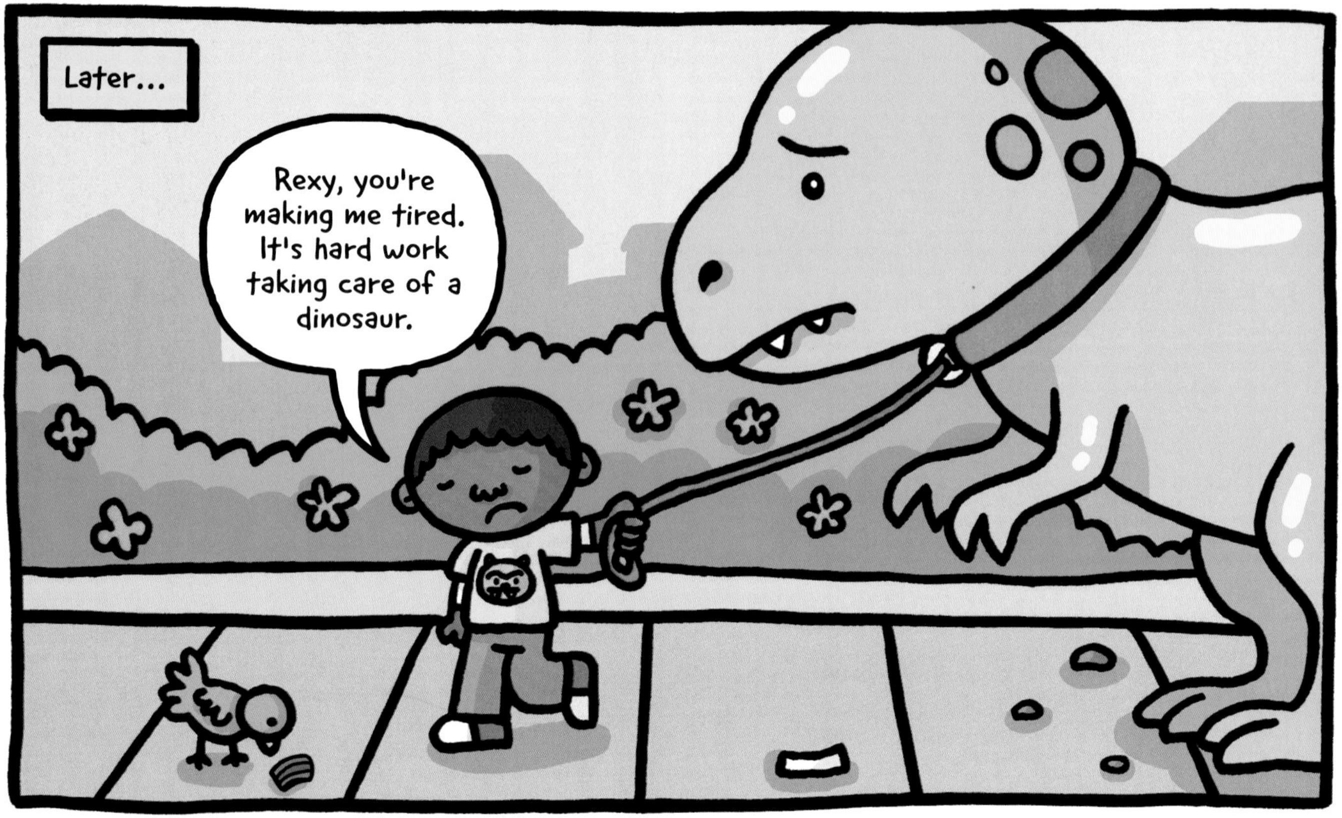
Later...
Rexy, you're making me tired. It's hard work taking care of a dinosaur.

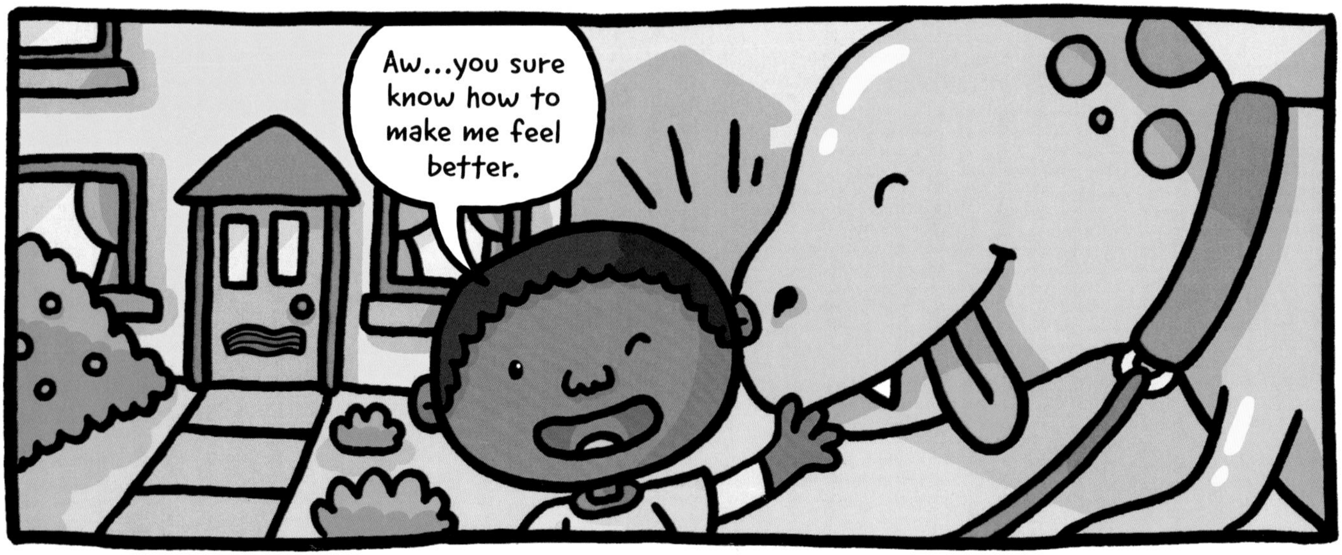
Aw...you sure know how to make me feel better.

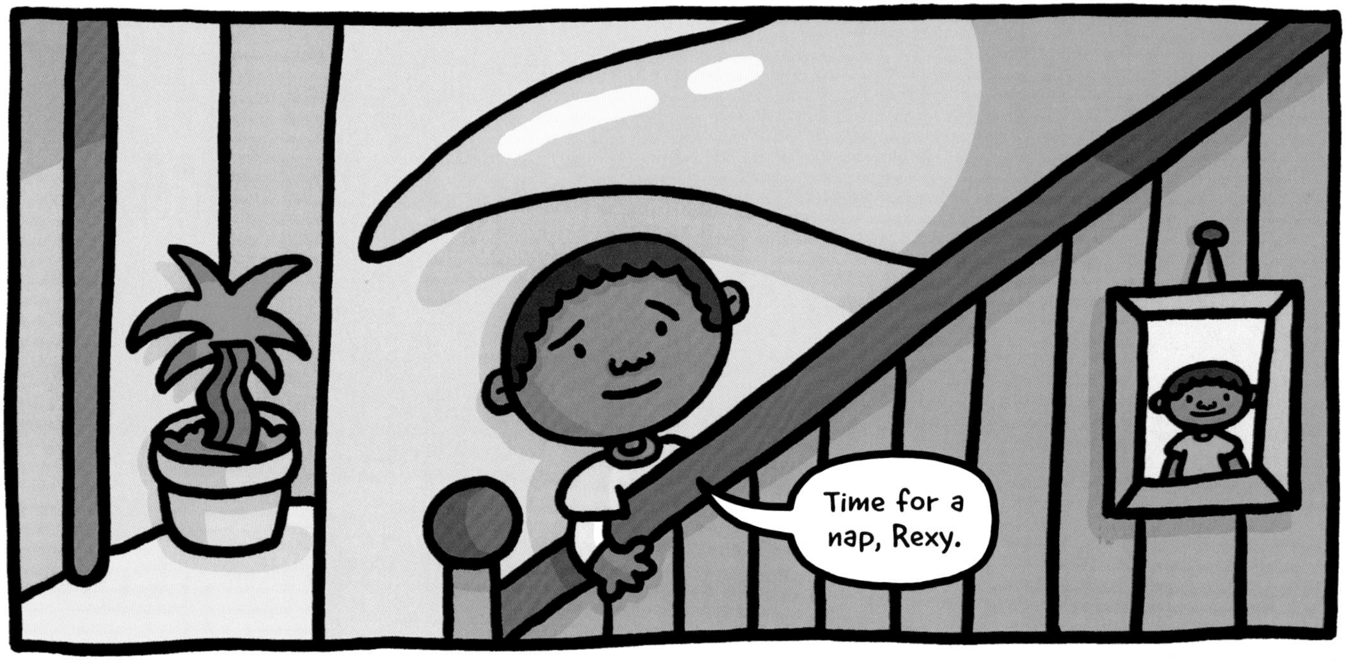
Time for a nap, Rexy.

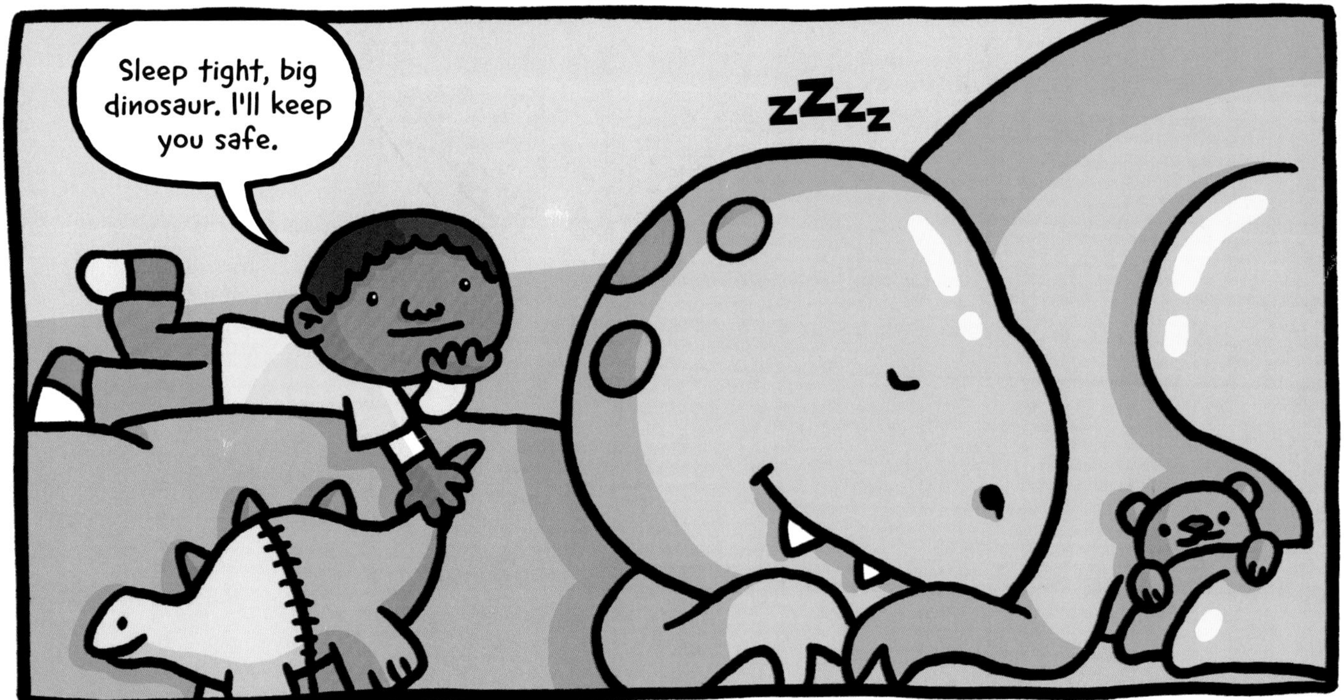
Sleep tight, big dinosaur. I'll keep you safe.
zZZz

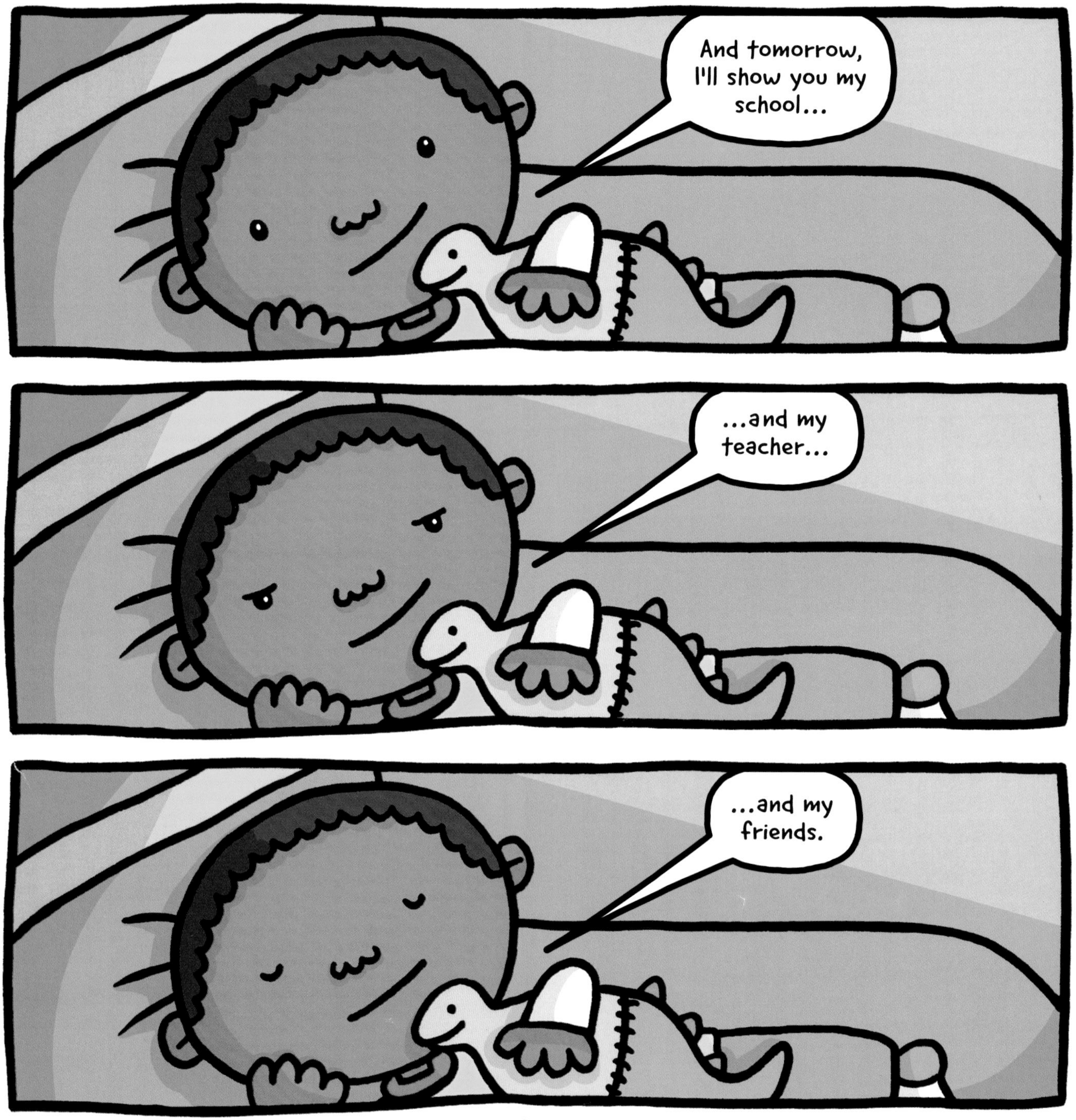
And tomorrow, I'll show you my school...
...and my teacher...
...and my friends.

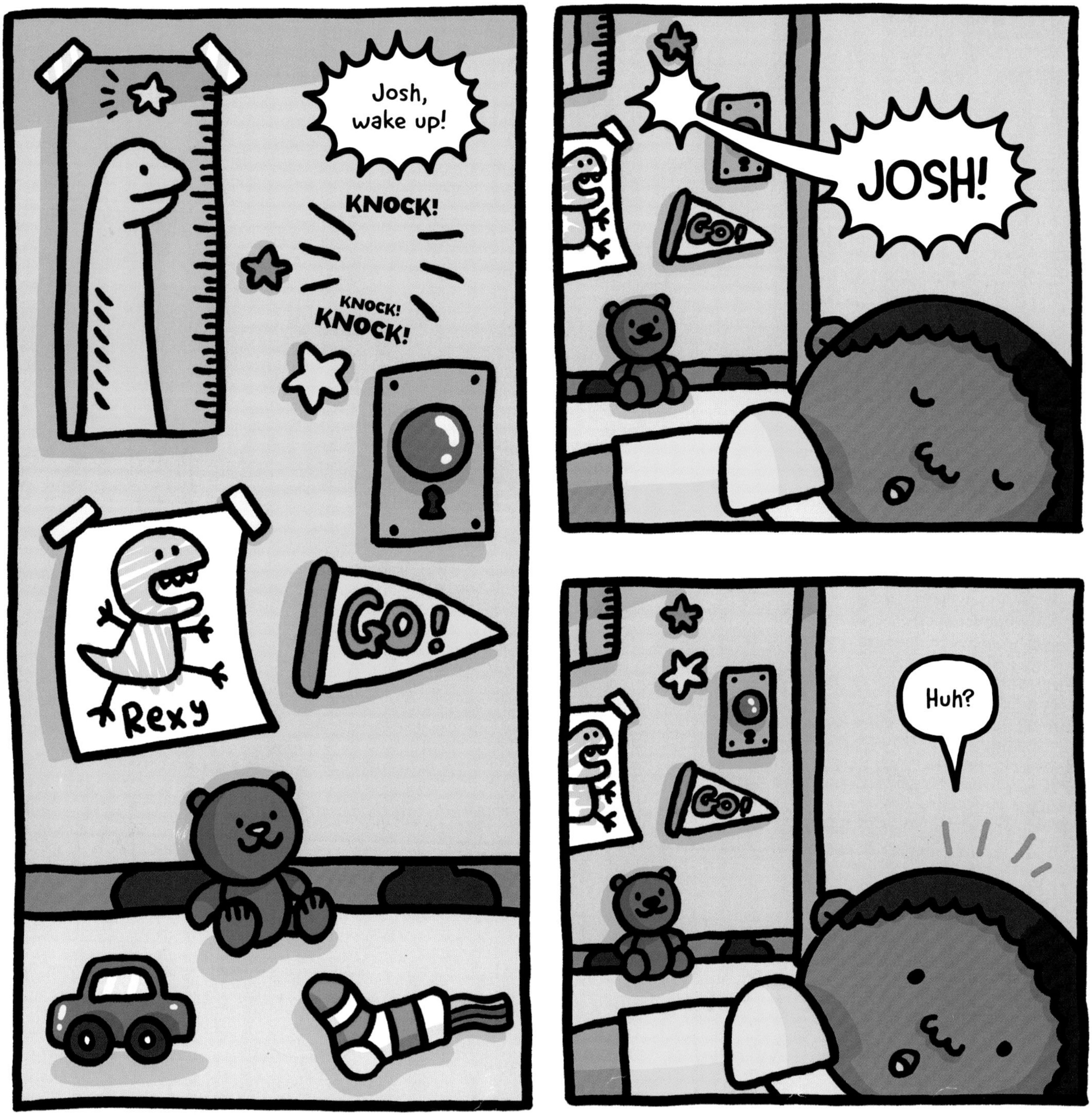
Josh, wake up!
KNOCK!
KNOCK! KNOCK!
Rexy
GO!
JOSH!
Huh?

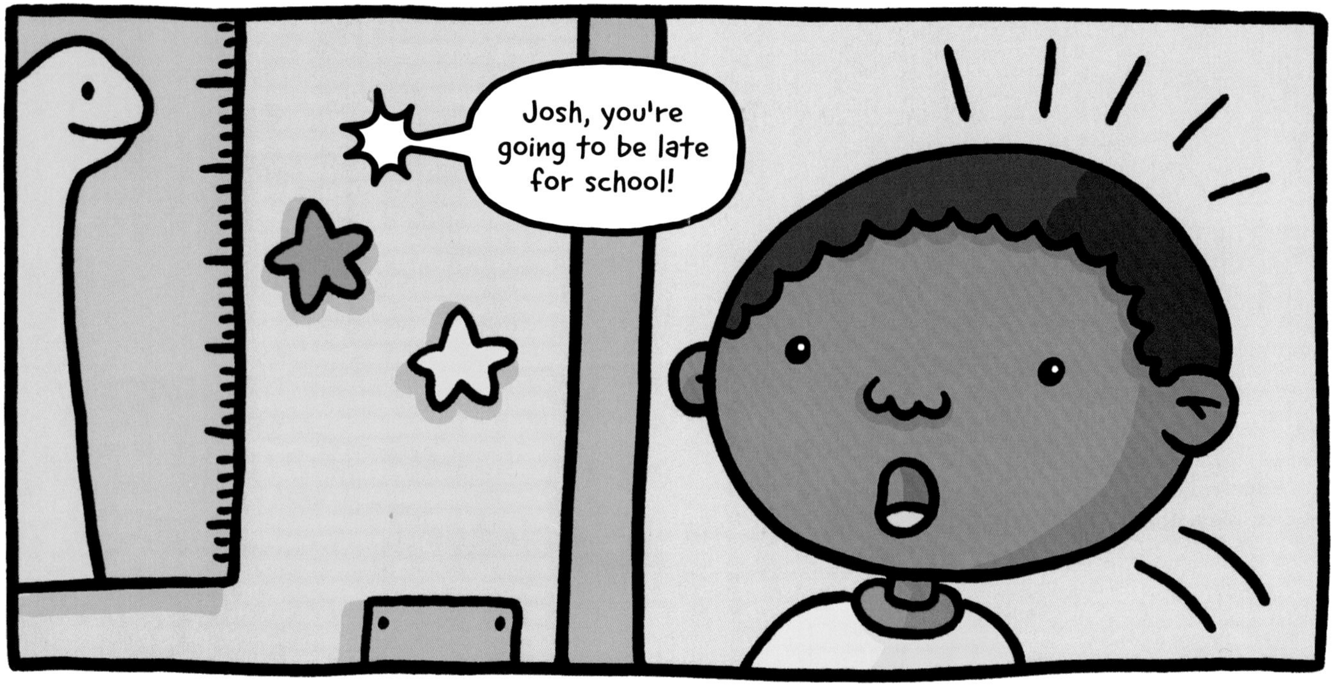
Josh, you're going to be late for school!

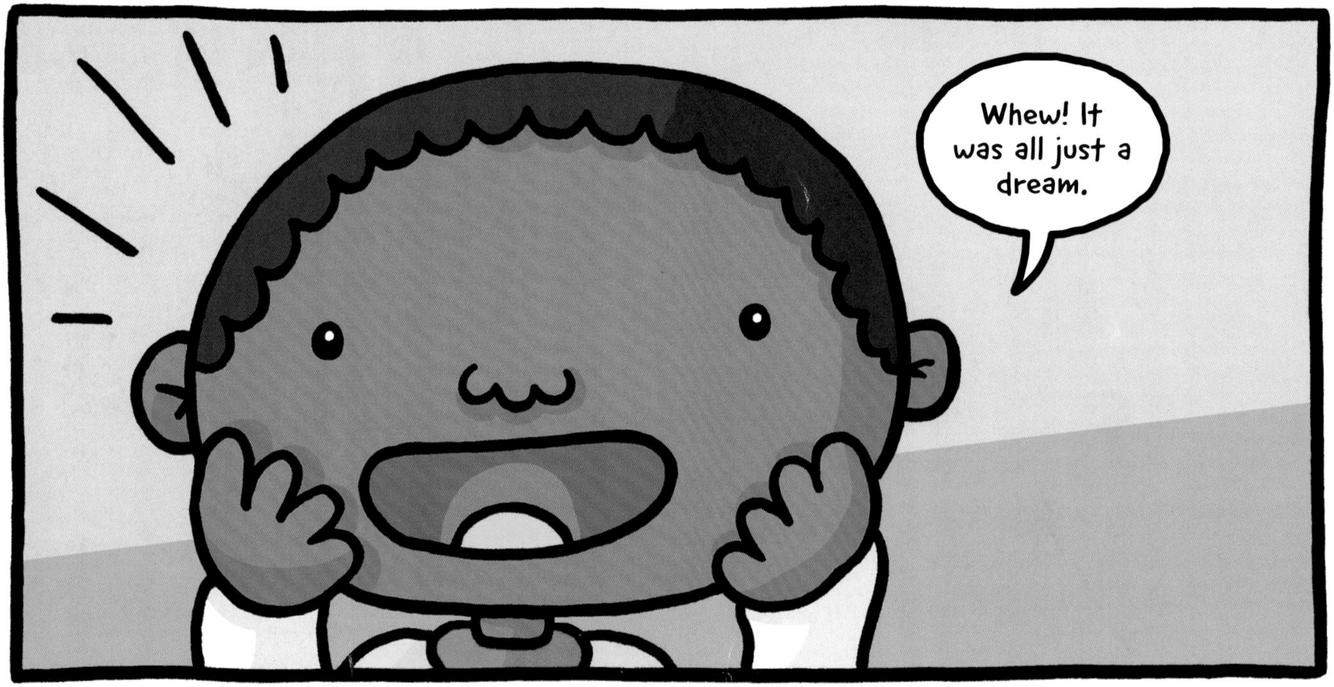
Whew! It was all just a dream.

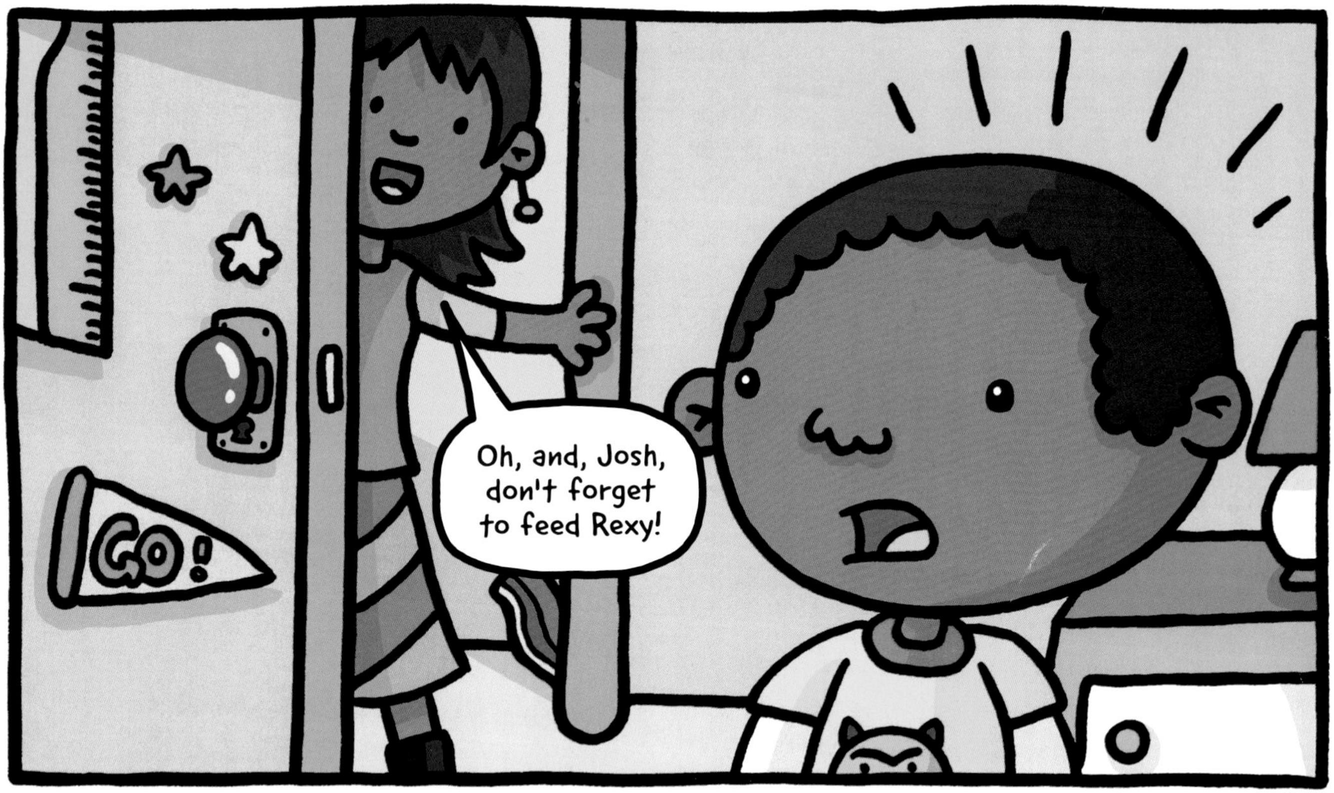
GO!
Oh, and, Josh, don't forget to feed Rexy!

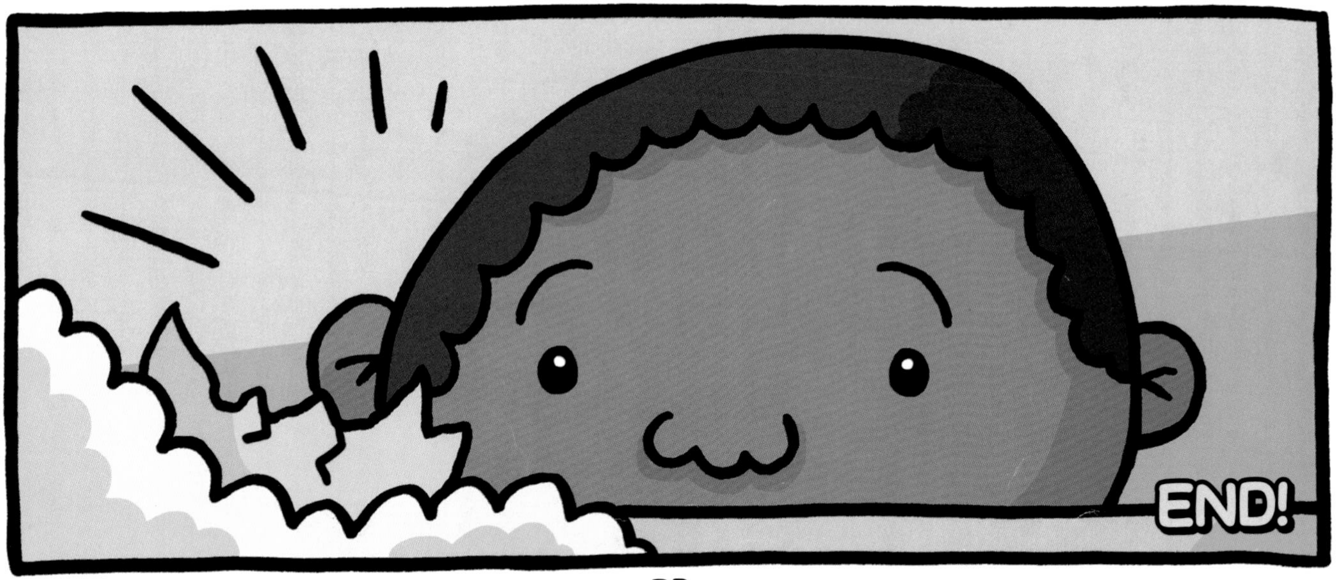
END!

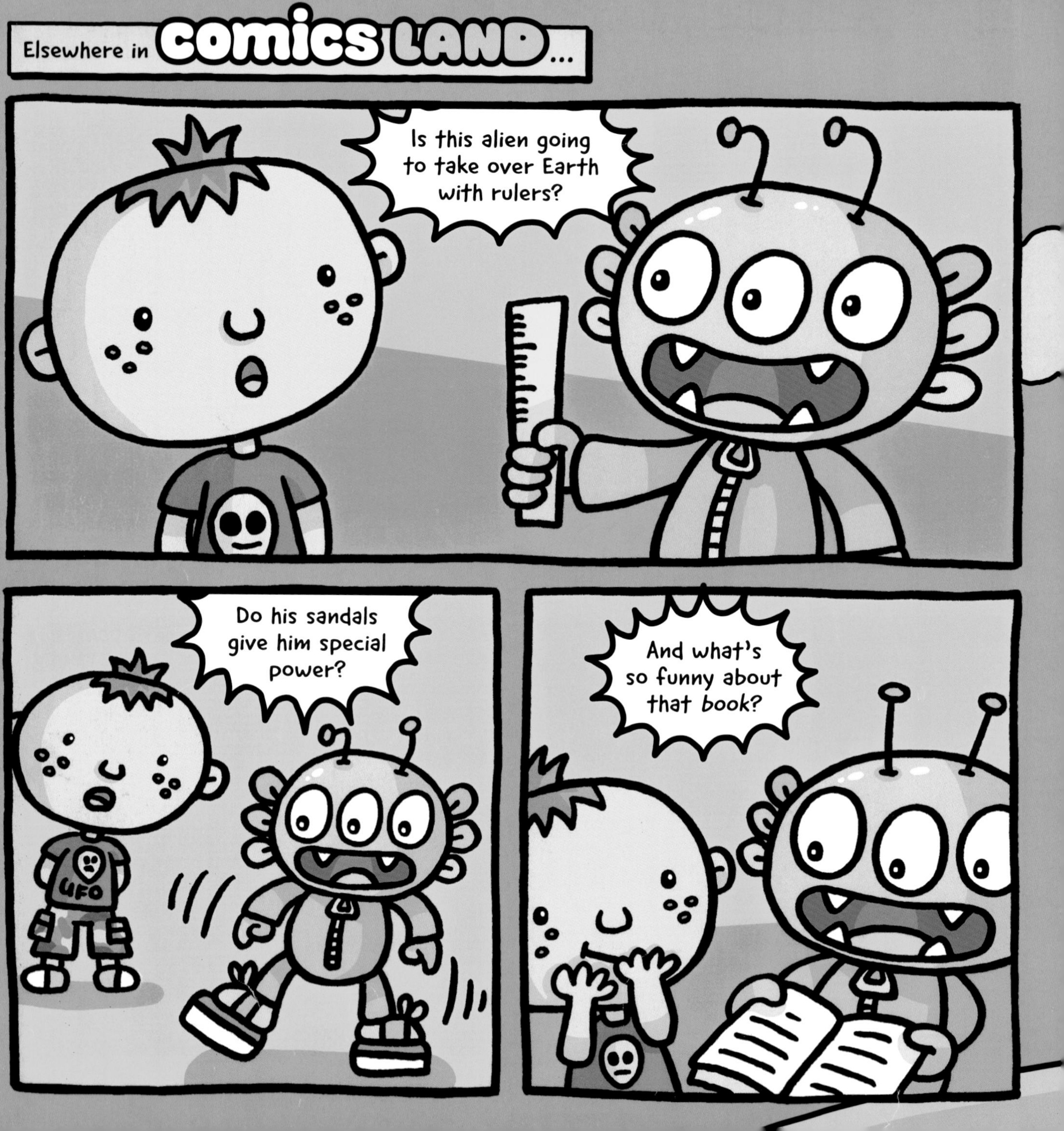
Elsewhere in COMICS LAND...
Is this alien going to take over Earth with rulers?
Do his sandals give him special power?
UFO
And what's so funny about that *book*?

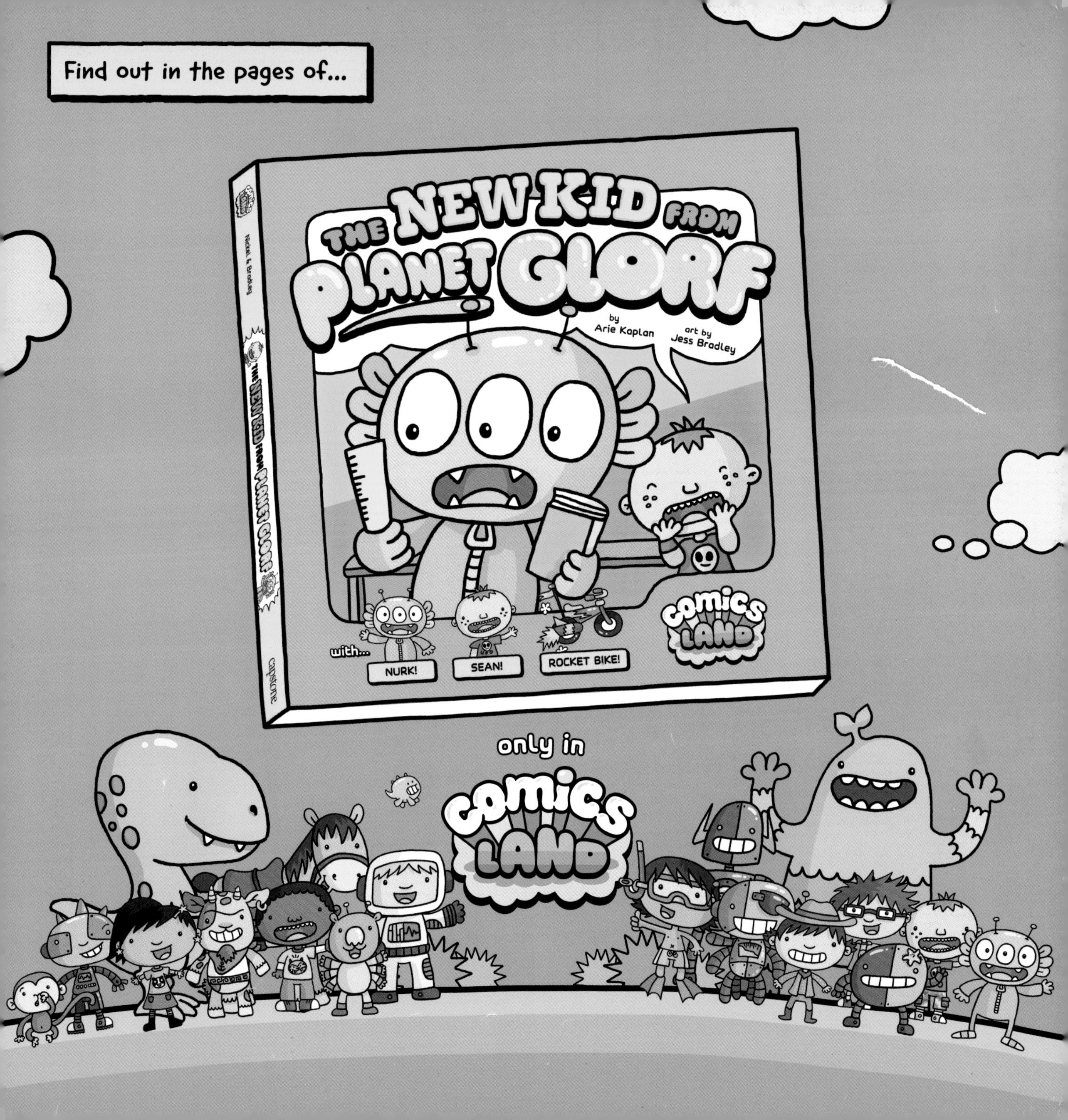
Find out in the pages of...
THE NEW KID FROM PLANET GLORF
by Arie Kaplan
art by Jess Bradley
with...
NURK!
SEAN!
ROCKET BIKE!
COMICS LAND
capstone
only in
COMICS LAND

DINOSAURS FOR BREAKFAST
PRESENTS

WORD POWER!

ATTACK (uh-TAK) — to try to hurt someone or something

BEASTS (BEESTS) — wild animals

EXTINCT (ek-STINGKT) — no longer exists

INDOOR (IN-dor) — used, done, or belonging inside

MUSEUM (myoo-ZEE-uhm) — a place where interesting objects of art, history, or science are displayed

TOENAIL (TOH-nayl) — a nail of a toe

TYRANNOSAURUS REX (ti-RAN-uh-sor-uhss REX) — a huge dinosaur that fed on meat and walked upright on its hind legs

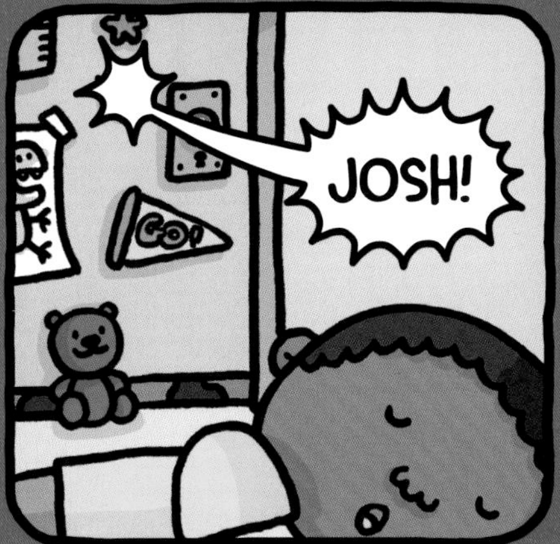
JOSH!

Who is talking to Josh in this panel? Where is the speaker standing?

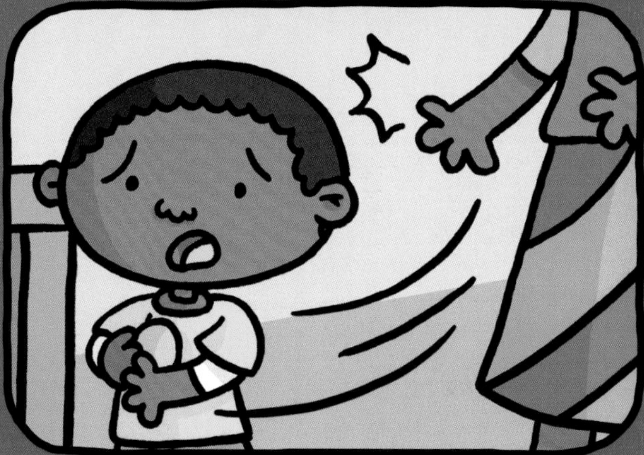

What do the black lines from Mom to Josh show? What does the star around Mom's hand show?

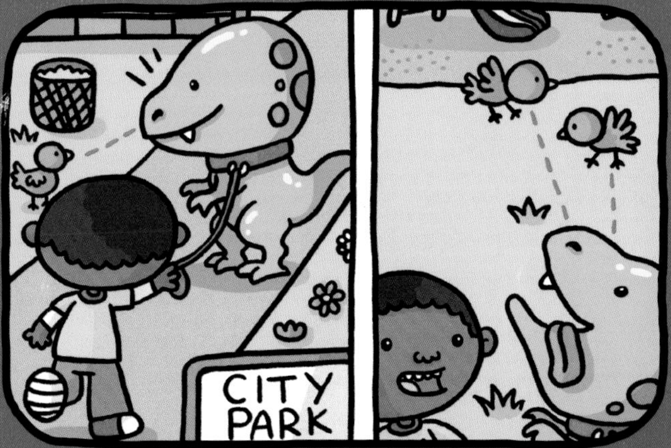
CITY PARK

Do you think Rexy is listening to Josh in this picture? What clues tell us what Rexy is thinking about?

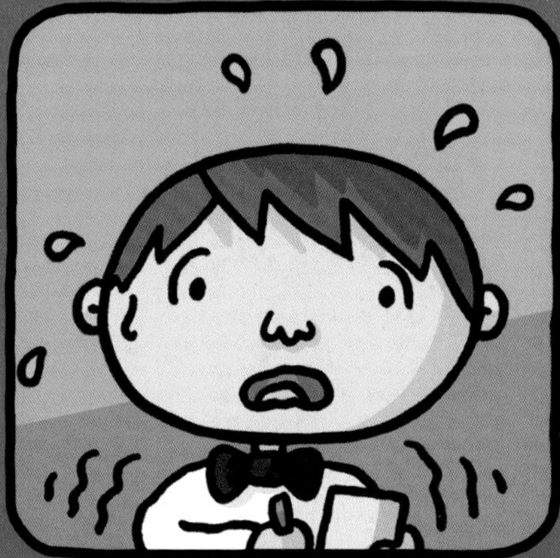

How does the waiter feel in the picture above? How do you know?

DINOSAURS FOR BREAKFAST PRESENTS

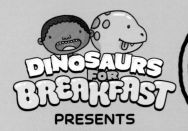

GAME TIME!

Every box, balloon, and burst in a comic has a special name and job. Can you match the object with its name?

A. SOUND BURST

B. SURPRISE LINES

C. EXCITEMENT BALLOON

D. WORD BALLOON

E. MOTION LINES

F. SOUND EFFECT

G. NARRATIVE BOX

H. THOUGHT BALLOON

1

2

3

4

5

6

7

POW!

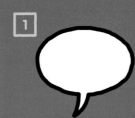

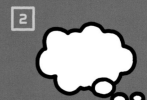

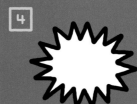

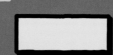

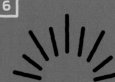

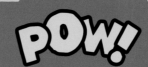

8

!

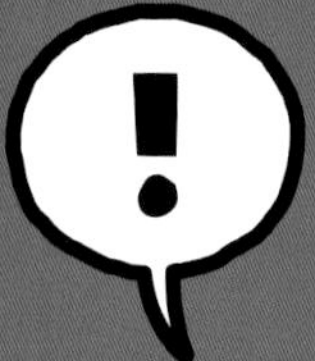

1=D, 2=H, 3=G, 4=A, 5=E, 6=B, 7=F, 8=C

Unscramble the letters to reveal words from the story.

1. LIEFD IRPT	5. ASBKERATF
2. OUDARINS	6. ZPIZA
3. GSEG	7. XREY
4. IXCETTN	8. DLISE

1=FIELD TRIP, 2=DINOSAUR, 3=EGGS, 4=EXTINCT, 5=BREAKFAST, 6=PIZZA, 7=REXY, 8=SLIDE

FIND THE BACON!

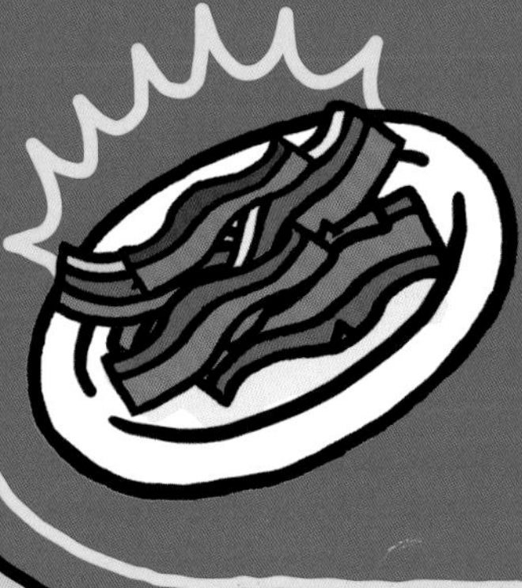

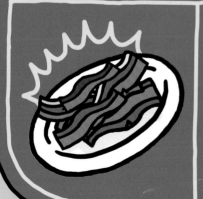

Bacon is a much better breakfast food than dinos! Fill your plate with the strips hidden throughout the book. There are **15** pieces in all.

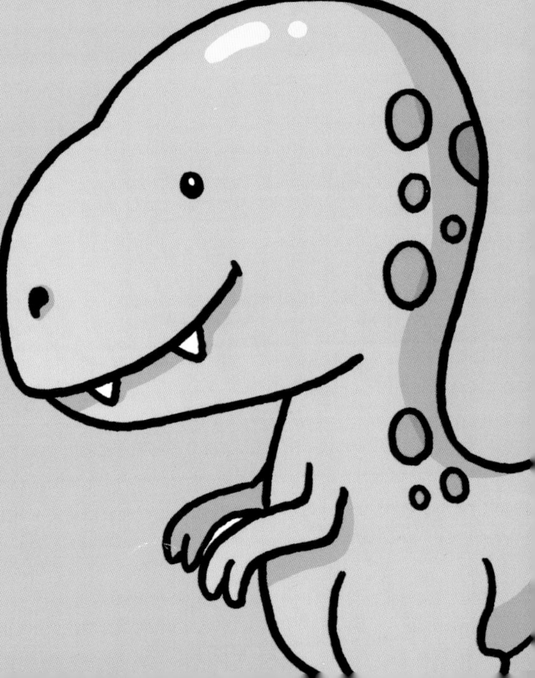

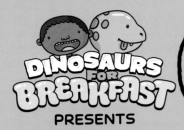

DINOSAURS FOR BREAKFAST PRESENTS

DRAW COMICS!

Want to make your own comic about Rexy? Start by learning to draw the little dinosaur. Comics Land artist Jess Bradley shows you how in six easy steps!

You will need:

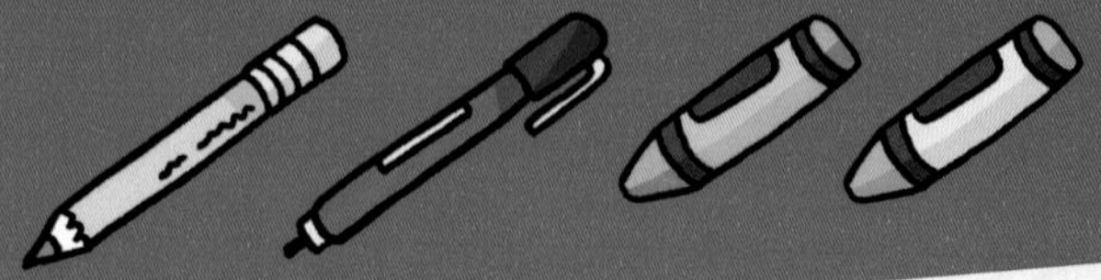

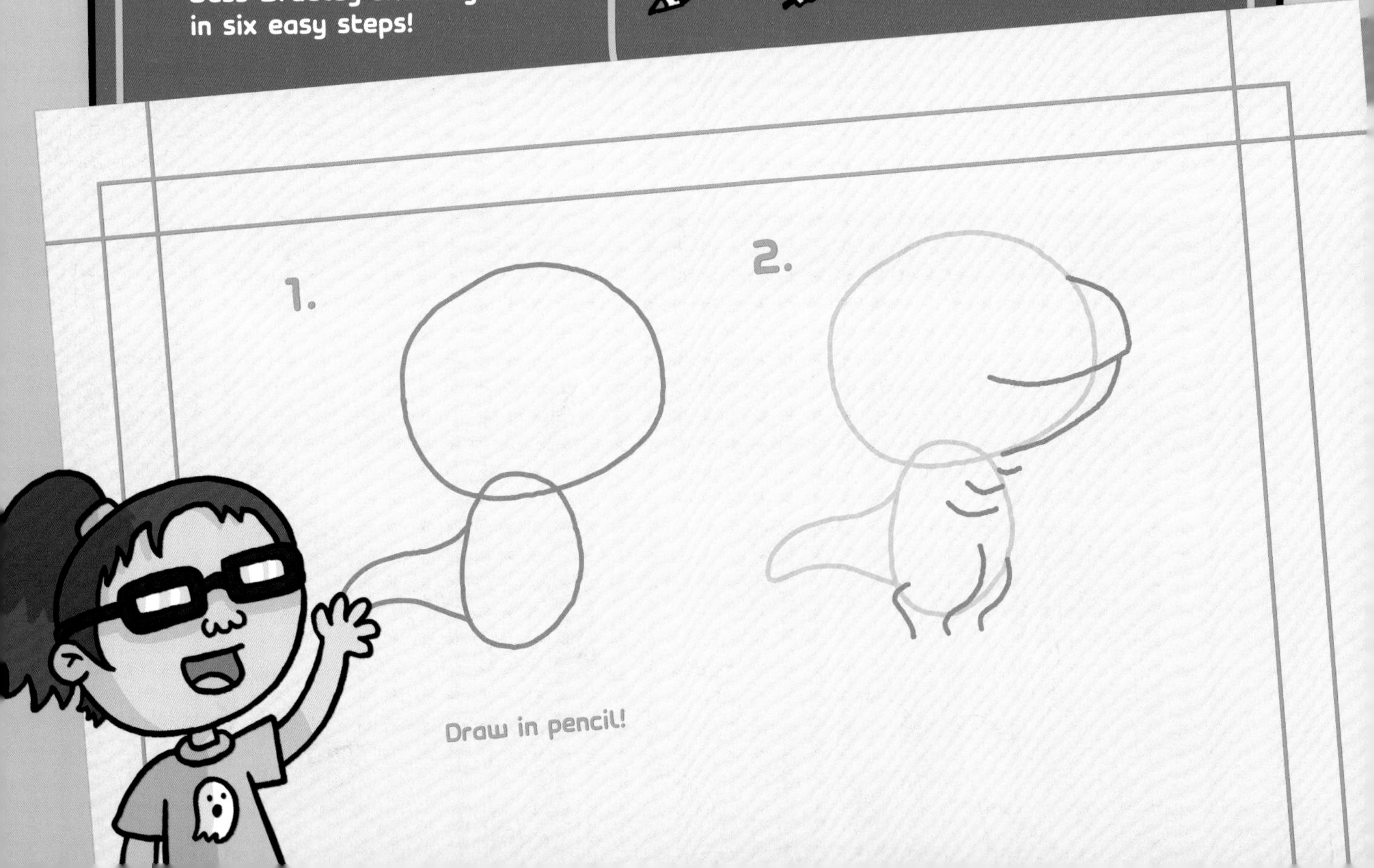
1.
2.
Draw in pencil!

3.

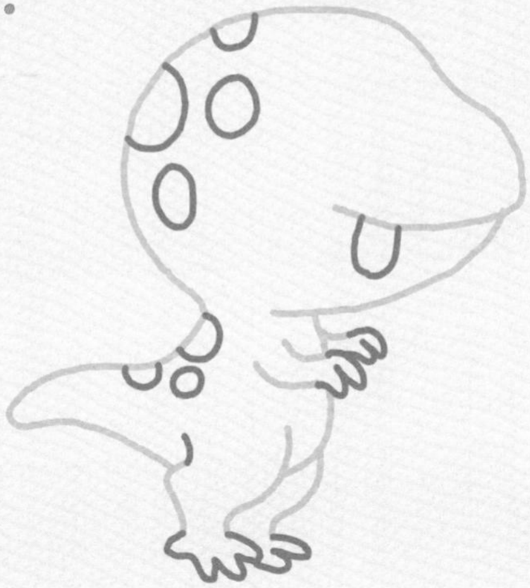

4.

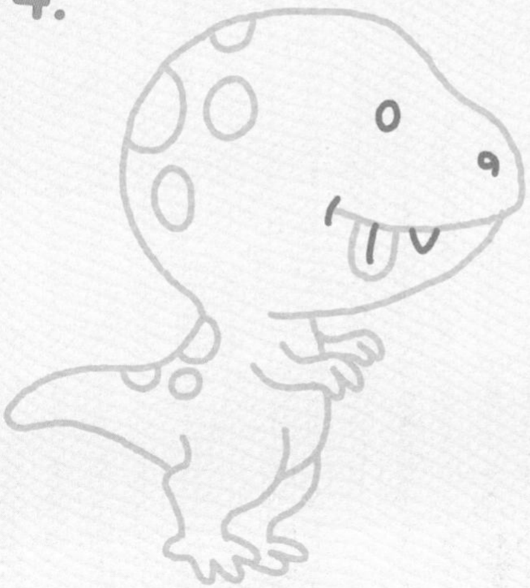

5.

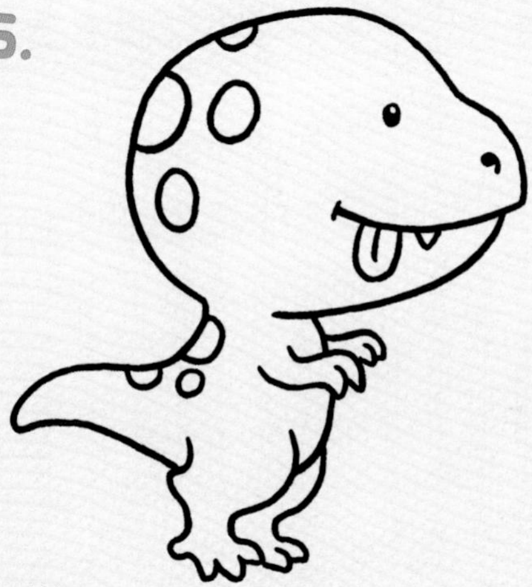

Outline in ink!

6.

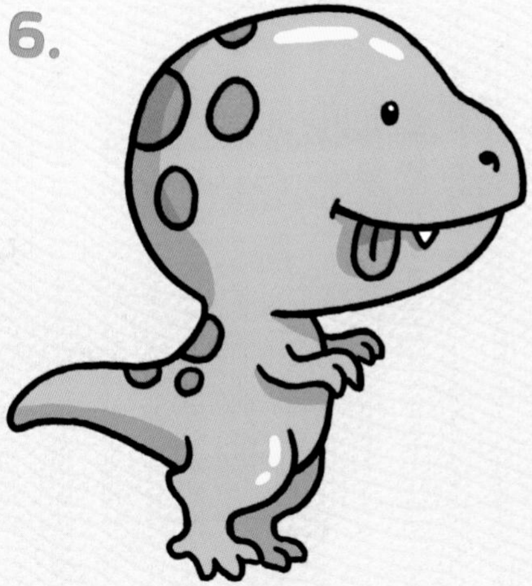

Color!

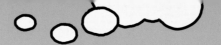

AMY J. LEMKE
WRITER

Amy J. Lemke is an Early Childhood Special Education teacher in Cambridge, Minnesota. She lives in Hugo, Minnesota, with her husband, Donnie, her puppy, Paulie, and her cat, Dylan. Amy enjoys riding bike, camping, traveling, and taking pictures.

JESS BRADLEY
ARTIST

Jess Bradley is an illustrator living and working in Bristol, England. She likes playing video games, painting, and watching bad films. Jess can also be heard to make a high-pitched "squeeeee" when excited, usually while watching videos clips of otters or getting new comics in the mail.

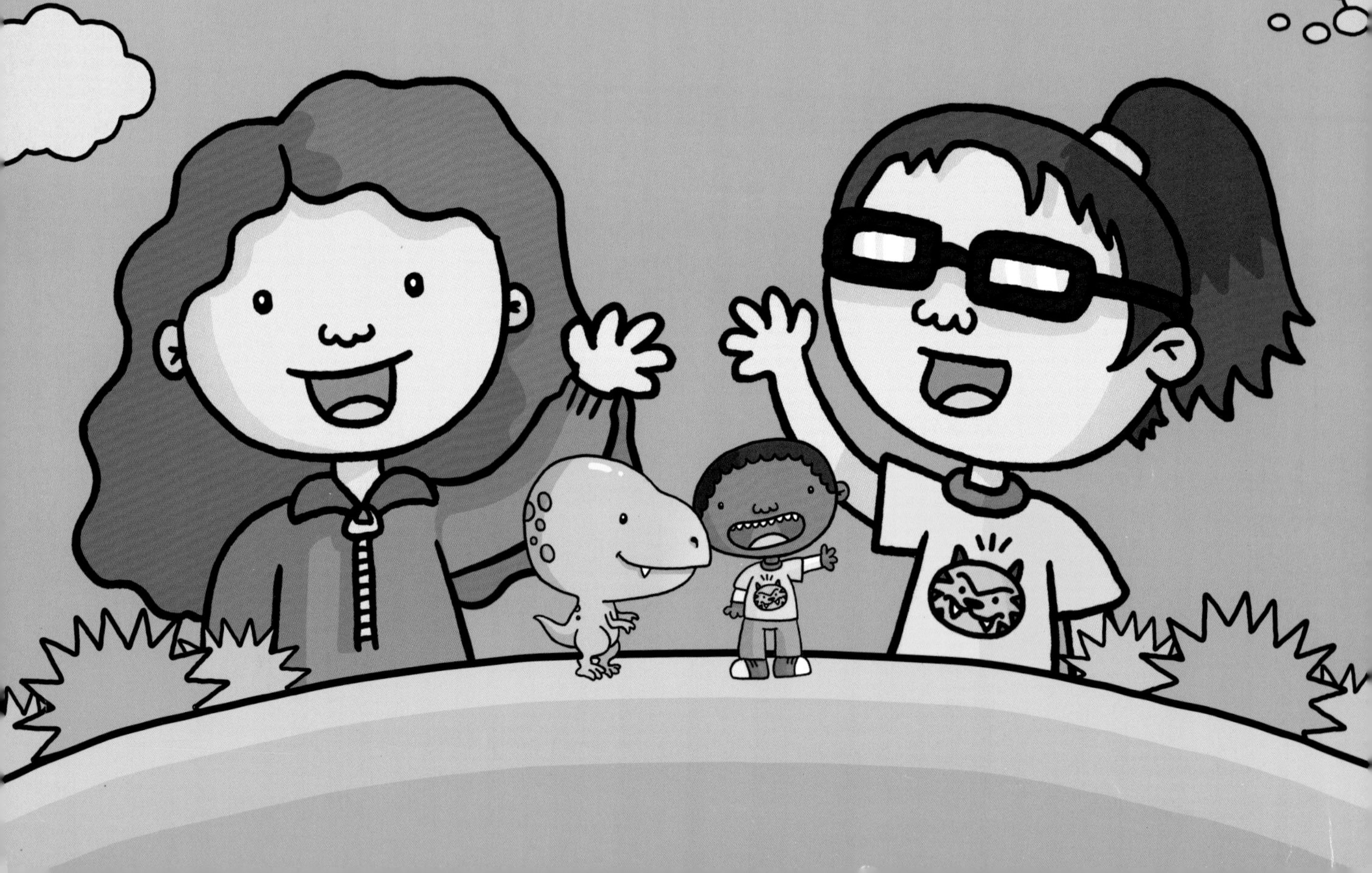